Ducky
Diary Two

**Other books by
Ann M. Martin**

P.S. Longer Letter Later
(written with Paula Danziger)
Leo the Magnificat
Rachel Parker, Kindergarten Show-off
Eleven Kids, One Summer
Ma and Pa Dracula
Yours Turly, Shirley
Ten Kids, No Pets
Slam Book
Just a Summer Romance
Missing Since Monday
With You and Without You
Me and Katie (the Pest)
Stage Fright
Inside Out
Bummer Summer

THE KIDS IN MS. COLMAN'S CLASS series
BABY-SITTERS LITTLE SISTER series
THE BABY-SITTERS CLUB mysteries
THE BABY-SITTERS CLUB series
CALIFORNIA DIARIES series

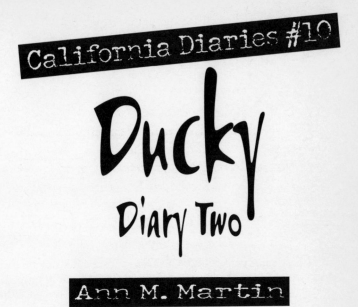

California Diaries #10

Ducky
Diary Two

Ann M. Martin

SCHOLASTIC INC.
New York Toronto London Auckland Sydney
Mexico City New Delhi Hong Kong

ISBN 0-590-02387-X

Copyright © 1998 by Ann M. Martin.
All rights reserved. Published by Scholastic Inc.
CALIFORNIA DIARIES is a trademark of Scholastic Inc.

12 11 10 9 8 7 6 5 4 3 2 1   8 9/9 0 1 2 3/0

Printed in the U.S.A.   40

First Scholastic printing, December 1998

The author gratefully acknowledges
Peter Lerangis
for his help in
preparing this manuscript.

Ducky the Fearless strikes again!

He leaves home late. He hits rush hour freeway traffic. He detours onto back roads through treacherous Windsor Hills and Inglewood, finally reaching the airport — and yes, ladies and gentlemen, he makes it to Gate 21 TWO MINUTES early! 5:35 for a 5:37 arriving flight.

Ducky the MIRACLE WORKER. Ducky the GOOD SON. HERE for his parents when they arrive from Ghana — on a SCHOOL NIGHT, the day before a math test.

Why? Because he WANTS TO. Because that's the kind of guy he is.

Then he checks the arrival screen. And he sees:

FLIGHT 407   1 HOUR LATE

(Cue laugh track.)

What a fool.

Okay. Let's analyze this, Ducky.

You might have known. This HAS happened before.

MOM AND DAD'S OVERSEAS FLIGHTS ARE ALMOST ALWAYS LATE.

You COULD HAVE CALLED IN ADVANCE TO CHECK. IF YOU KNEW, YOU WOULDN'T HAVE PANICKED AND RUSHED.

Now, SUDDENLY, YOU HAVE TIME TO KILL AND NOTHING TO DO. AND THIS WOULD BE A PERFECT OPPORTUNITY FOR SOME BADLY NEEDED MATH REVIEW. BUT YOU CAN'T DO IT BECAUSE — IN YOUR HURRY — YOU FORGOT YOUR REVIEW MATERIAL.

AND WHY ARE YOU HERE ALONE TO PICK UP YOUR LUCKY PARENTS ON THE DAY BEFORE A MATH TEST?

WELL, THAT BREAKS DOWN INTO TWO QUESTIONS:

1. WHY ARE YOU HERE? BECAUSE TED, OLDER AND MORE BELOVED SON, COULDN'T BE. YOU SEE, DUCKY, HE'S A COLLEGE BOY. YOU MAY HAVE HOMEWORK, BUT HE HAS A COURSE LOAD.

2. WHY ARE YOU HERE ALONE? BECAUSE NONE OF YOUR FRIENDS WOULD COME ALONG TO KEEP YOU COMPANY.

→ NOT JAY, FORMERLY KNOWN AS JASON, ONCE YOUR BEST FRIEND AND NOW A MEMBER OF THE VISTA SCHOOL CRO MAGS, DEDICATED TO THE GRUNT-AND-SNORT SCHOOL OF SOCIAL BEHAVIOR. JAY'S HELPFUL COMMENT? "COME ON, DUCKSTER, THEY'RE OLD ENOUGH TO GET HOME BY THEMSELVES." WHICH, YOU HAVE TO ADMIT, ISN'T A BAD POINT.

→ Not Alex. Too depressed, of course. (Which doesn't surprise you. But because you're best friends, and because you've been HELPING him through the gloomy state he's in, you still hoped he might come along. No such luck.)

→ Not Sunny, even though she's ALWAYS looking for excuses to get away from her house. She's busy tonight — with what or whom she won't say, but you know her slippery-cute tone of voice translates into: NEW BOYFRIEND. Which means you may not see her for awhile . . . until, of course, this guy turns out to be just like the others, and she comes back to cry on your shoulder. And that's FINE because Sunny needs you, she's freaking out because of her mom's cancer, and the boyfriends are a way of escaping reality.

You understand everyone's excuses, because that's what you do best, Ducky. You think of others first. And second. And third.

Somewhere down the list of concerns — oh, maybe near the price of asparagus and the political situation in Norway — is YOU.

I.

Say I when you mean I, Ducky. Don't hide. When am I going to learn?

Maybe Jay is right. You COULD have let Mom and Dad take a car service.

~~You~~ I should think about ~~yourself~~ myself for a change.

MYSELF. ME.

God, I hate the way that sounds.

THREE HOURS LATER
In Which Ducky, Still Waiting,
with Nothing Else to Do,
Sees Scenes from His Life
Reenacted All Around Him

For example, you look around the arrival gate and see:

→ The toddler, strapped into her stroller and crying madly, ignoring her drippy ice-cream cone as a DC-10 rises into the smog outside the window. Boy, do you remember THAT feeling.

→ The two little boys at Gate 22 running into a crowd of arriving passengers and being scooped up by a tired but happy businessman. The mom joins them, making a four-person sandwich, and you can almost hear them squeal, "We're the ham and cheese, you're the bread!" — but no, that's what YOU used to say. It's only a memory. But you can taste the hope and excitement in the air. You know what those boys are thinking right now. Today Daddy's home for good. Today everything will be normal again.

Maybe for them it's true. Maybe THEIR parents aren't professors-slash-international business consultants like yours.

For YOU, Ducky, things were never normal. Because Mom and Dad always had another trip. And when they were gone, you worried they'd forget you, or find new kids to love, or just plain never come back. You counted the days on a calendar and looked at atlases and encyclopedias, hoping to see Paris through Mom's and Dad's eyes, or Boston or Abu Dhabi or Toronto or Sri Lanka. And you wondered why you couldn't have gone along too and WHAT you did wrong and HOW you could make them want to stay home next time — IF I CLEAN MY ROOM EVERY DAY, IF

I STOP YELLING AT MY BROTHER, IF I GET STRAIGHT A's...

The trips eventually became a part of life, expected, unavoidable, like breakfast and homework. The fears became hidden away like a scabbed-over wound — and soon even the scab was gone, leaving only a scar.

Scars protect. Scars heal. But they're markers too, reminders of what's underneath.

So when you see that toddler and those boys, the scar stretches. You feel a little of the old pain.

And you ask some of the old questions: What will Mom and Dad be like when they arrive? Will they be happy to see you? How long will they stay this time? Until the spring? Until the new year, at least?

The difference between now and then is that at 16, you KNOW some of the answers.

You know to settle for reality. Which isn't too bad, really. Soon 121 Sherwood Road will look and smell the way it used to. Like a house with a real family in it.

Still, you want something MORE.

An edge. An electricity.

Something.

And you know you won't get it.

9:07 P.M.

The 5:37 has arrived.

MUCH LATER

After an Evening of Song, Dance, and Laughter

Well, maybe not dance.

Definitely not song.

Laughter? Uh, well...

Let's just say it's been a weird night.

Starting with the arrival of the plane.

The Reunion of the McCraes

Based on a True Story

Act 1, Scene 1:

SETTING:

Los Angeles International Airport, 9:10 P.M.,

December 1. Great hubbub at Gate 21. Passengers

EMERGE FROM THE PLANE INTO THE WAITING CROWD.
FAMILIES HUG AND CRY. BOYFRIENDS AND GIRLFRIENDS ARE
LOST IN EACH OTHER'S EMBRACES. DUCKY, A NONDESCRIPT,
DARK-HAIRED 16-YEAR-OLD, CRANES HIS NECK. HE SEES:

CUT TO:

A TANNED, TRIM, MIDDLE-AGED COUPLE WALKING OUT
OF THE GATE. THEY ARE STRUGGLING WITH THEIR CARRY-ON
LUGGAGE.

DUCKY LOOKS AWAY.

THEN HE DOES A DOUBLE TAKE. THEY'RE HIS PARENTS.
HE DIDN'T RECOGNIZE THEM AT FIRST. WAS IT THEIR TANS?
THEIR WEIGHT LOSS? OR HAS IT REALLY BEEN SO LONG SINCE
HE LAST SAW THEM?

DUCKY'S HEART IS BEATING FASTER. HE SMILES. HE
WAVES AND CALLS OUT THEIR NAMES.

FATHER AND MOTHER TURN. THEY SPOT DUCKY
ACROSS THE MULTITUDES.

[SWELLING MUSIC.]

DUCKY [ENTHUSIASTICALLY, ARMS WIDE, BIG SMILE]: HI!

MOTHER [WITH QUICK KISS ON D'S CHEEK]: THANK YOU
FOR COMING, SWEETIE. WOULD YOU HELP WITH THE CARRY-ONS?

FATHER [PUTTING GARMENT BAG OVER D'S
OUTSTRETCHED ARM, WHICH IS ALREADY HOLDING M'S BAG]:
WHAT A TRIP. GLAD YOU'RE HERE. HEAVY ENOUGH?

D [SAGGING UNDER THE WEIGHT]: UH, FINE.

M: WHERE'S TED?

D: Studying.

F: At least SOMEBODY's working. Heh-heh. Let's get our luggage.

M & F walk briskly ahead toward baggage claim. D lags behind, loaded down with luggage. Dumbfounded. Drooping. Dodging and ducking through the crowd.

D [thinking, in a voice-over]: <u>They're tired. It was a long flight. So they're not gooey and emotional. That's not their style anyway. Deal with it.</u>

M: Are you still with us, Ducky?

D [voice-over]: <u>Ducky?</u>

He smiles. F and M sometimes still use his nickname. It's a touching moment. It sounds so natural, so RIGHT, in a funny way. A glimmer of happiness.

Which ends as he collides with a man in a Hawaiian shirt.

CUT. CHANGE REEL

You reach the baggage claim bruised but alive. You drop the carry-ons. Mom and Dad are looking to the place where the suitcases will first appear.

"How was the trip?" you ask.

Mom begins, "Well, I made great progress on my paper...."

You hear about the water level of the Volta

River. The price fluctuations of manganese ore and bauxite. The condition of the cacao crop and its effects on the coastal Ashanti people.

Right.

"Didn't you do anything FUN?" you ask.

They don't answer. They're distracted by the carousel, which is now going around without their luggage. So Dad begins to worry aloud that his stuff has been stolen or switched onto a flight to Katmandu, where some lucky Sherpa will soon be leading mountain treks dressed in his Brooks Brothers seersucker suit. And you don't want him to make a scene, but there's no way to stop him — he's off yelling at some skycap, threatening to sue the airline, when

HALLELUJAH!

The suitcases arrive. But now Dad's caught in one of his funks, so you try to be lighthearted and cheerful as you drag the luggage to the airport doors. You run to the lot, fetch the car, and load everything into the trunk. You hand Dad the keys, but he shakes his head. "No, you go ahead."

You turn toward Mom. She's already sliding into the backseat.

YOU'RE driving, Ducky. No way out.

The Torture Begins.

As you pull away from the curb, Dad STOMPS on an imaginary brake. As you approach the crosswalk, he YELLS at you to watch out for the pedestrians. He GASPS at near-accidents that are (let's face it) all in his mind.

Soon you're crawling along the freeway at five miles UNDER the speed limit, eyes ahead, teeth clenched, knuckles gripping the steering wheel. Mom exclaims how nice it is to be back home, but all you can see out the window is smoggy, gray Culver City, and you think either she's lying or Ghana must be pretty dismal, when suddenly she asks, "So...how are YOU, sweetie?"

YOU.

What a shock.

There's so much you want to say — your schoolwork, your new friendships, your job at Winslow Books — and everything rushes out at once, but nothing makes much sense.

Dad interrupts you. "What about Mrs. Winslow?" he mumbles. "Is she...?"

"Still alive, yup," you reply, and you HATE the way the words sound — a quick update, just the headlines — implying all is well, when in reality it's NOT — Sunny's mom is DYING and Sunny's going through her own private hell. But you CAN'T go into that or into

ANYTHING IMPORTANT, BECAUSE DAD IS TELLING YOU TO BEAR LEFT, SLOW DOWN, USE YOUR SIGNALS — AND WHEN YOUR EXIT FINALLY APPEARS, YOU WANT TO VEER ONTO A SIDE STREET, PARK THE CAR, AND WALK HOME.

BUT INSTEAD YOU OBEDIENTLY DRIVE TO YOUR HOUSE, THEN TOTE THE BAGGAGE INSIDE WHILE MOM AND DAD GIVE TED A BIG, EMOTIONAL GREETING, AND TED SEEMS ACTUALLY INTERESTED IN THE NEWS ABOUT BAUXITE (THE FAKER), WHICH IS WHY THEY ADORE HIM SO MUCH MORE THAN YOU (DUCKY, YOU DIDN'T WRITE THAT).

SOON DAD'S COMPLAINING. THE TV'S BEEN MOVED TO THE WRONG SIDE OF THE LIVING ROOM. THERE'S NO REAL FOOD IN THE FRIDGE. A SLICE OF PIZZA HAS SLIPPED BETWEEN THE FRIDGE AND THE COUNTER, SOMEHOW UNSEEN BY YOU AND TED.

MOM'S WANDERING AROUND THE HOUSE, RUNNING HER FINGERS ALONG THE COUNTERS, GAZING THROUGH THE WINDOWS, AS IF VISITING A PLACE IN A DREAM. YOU TRY NOT TO LOOK AT HER FACE AS SHE DISCOVERS A SOCK BEHIND THE SOFA...AND THE SMUDGE MARKS ON THE CEILING THAT TED'S FRIENDS MADE, PASSING AROUND THE BASKETBALL INSIDE THE HOUSE.

THIS IS NOT WHAT YOU EXPECTED. YOU'VE DONE FIVE LOADS OF LAUNDRY. WASHED ALL THE DISHES. SWEPT THE KITCHEN FLOOR. SCRUBBED THE BATHTUB. TAKEN OUT THE GARBAGE.

You're proud of yourself. Proud of Ted too (even though he did one-tenth the work you did, but hey, anything's an improvement). You thought Mom and Dad would be happy. You thought they'd appreciate the effort.

Oh, well.

You're in your room now, after a very late dinner, door closed. Ducky's Cave.

You can hear Mom and Dad in their room, unpacking, grumbling. The 24-hour news radio station is droning in the background. (That is such a DAD thing.)

You feel cooped up.

A day ago, you felt as if the WHOLE HOUSE was your room. Now you're back to these four walls again.

It's THEIR house now. No more dropping your clothes on the floor and picking them up whenever. No more leaving the dishes in the sink overnight. No more loud music — YOUR music, YOUR radio stations — whenever you want.

You may have gained a family, Ducky boy.

But you've lost your freedom.

Wednesday, 12/2
Bleary-eyed in Homeroom

You wake up to the smell of grilled ham-and-cheese sandwiches. Mom and Dad are in the kitchen, eating lunch. At 7:00 A.M.

They're still on Ghana time.

They stayed up all night, noticing things wrong with the house. Things Ted and you "neglected." Now — while you're still half asleep — they present you with a handy list of questions:

Did we renew their magazine subscriptions? Did we tip the gardener? Did we pick up the dry cleaning? Did we turn over their car's engine regularly?

TURN OVER THE ENGINE?

Ted and you sit there in disbelief.

Afterward, you both hop into YOUR cars and take off.

You're a little early for school, so you take the scenic route, past Las Palmas County Park. That makes you unwind a bit. You think about how you used to practically live there on the weekends, doing nothing — just skipping stones and wasting hours with Alex.

That thought makes you smile.

Then you think of the Ghost of Alex Present.

You remember he was absent from school yesterday. So you take a detour and stop by his house.

His mom's car is gone. She's already left for work. With Paula, whose school starts earlier than ours.

You ring. And ring. After about five minutes he opens the door, his eyes half closed. He is dressed in a T-shirt and boxers. Sleepwear.

You ask if he's sick.

"No," he replies. "Why?"

"Last time I looked, it was a school day," you say.

It's supposed to be a joke. But Alex just grumbles something under his breath and walks into the house.

You follow. He disappears into his room for another five minutes. When he emerges, he has put on long pants. Same T-shirt, same sleep-hair.

"You're going like THAT?" you ask.

He just shrugs.

Now it's getting late, so you rush him out to the car. "Alex, what would you have done if I hadn't picked you up?"

"I don't know."

"Where were you yesterday?"

"Here. Around." No apology. No explanation.

"Alex, you've missed A LOT of school lately."

"Yeah. So?"

"So? I'd prefer to have my best friend remain in MY GRADE next year."

You can see his lips curling upward into something like a smile. He repeats "Next year" under his breath.

As if you're a total idiot for bringing it up.

You remind yourself HE'S DEPRESSED. That's why he's in therapy. Until he recovers, he needs companionship, UNDERSTANDING. He's not getting it from any other kids in school. Not even from Jay, who used to be one of his best buddies. So it's up to you, Ducky. Be cool, you think.

You ignore the comment. Drop the topic of discussion. Tell him about your last 24 hours — the gory details of the McCrae family reentry period — until you realize you're talking his ear off.

You take a deep breath. "So. What do you think? Why do these trips get HARDER?"

Alex looks at you blankly. "Huh?"

"My parents' trips?"

"Oh. Did they come back or something?"

"Alex, didn't you HEAR what I said?"

You are stopped at a red light now. Alex looks confused. "Sorry," he says. "I'm spacing out."

So you patiently repeat yourself.

"They weren't on vacation, Ducky," he says. "They were working."

"I KNOW that."

"People get tired and cranky when they work hard. Plus the travel. The time change. You'd be the same too. They'll sleep. Then they'll come around."

Good point. A very Alex perspective.

"How about you?" you ask.

"How about me what?"

"Are you 'coming around' too?"

"From what?"

"You know. Your bad feelings."

DEPRESSION. Why can't you say the word? You had to drag him home drunk and soaking wet from Jay's party after he'd locked himself in the bathroom and passed out. You had to call Dr. Welsch in the middle of the night and tell him what happened. Alex KNOWS you know. So why beat around the bush?

"I'm cool," Alex says.

"Dr. Welsch helping you?"

"No."

You can't tell if Alex means NO, Dr. Welsch isn't helping him or NO, he isn't seeing Dr. Welsch anymore.

You are pulling into a parking space by now.

And Alex leaves the car before you can ask.

The Case of the Missing Friend Continues

WHAT is going on?

You're walking in the hallway after homeroom. You happen to glance through the door to the parking lot and you spot him outside, staring at the school, hands in pockets. You wave, but he doesn't see you. He just turns and walks away.

He's hidden by all the SUVs, so no one else notices him.

You run outside, calling his name. He turns and says hey, Ducky, what's up — like it's a totally normal thing to be outside when you're supposed to be in chemistry class.

"Chemistry?" he repeats. He has NO CLUE.

"Yeah...chemistry!" You're quick. PERFECT imitation. Sky Masterson, Guys and Dolls. Which you and Alex listened to at least a million times when you were kids. It's his cue to start singing "I'll Know" à la Alex, WAY out of tune — but he just nods and heads back toward school.

Mr. O'Toole is not happy to see you. When he finds out Alex has no notebook OR textbook, he gives a big lecture on RESPONSIBILITY.

Alex is in another world, playing with a rubber band.

Mr. O'Toole moves right up close to him, waves his hands, and does a little soft-shoe. When Alex finally looks up, O'Toole says, "Whew, I'm glad THAT worked. Next I was going to have to do a striptease."

Typical O'Toole humor. The class is cracking up. You're hearing whispered comments about Alex and you KNOW they think he's a druggie or an alcoholic AND MAYBE HE IS, you don't know, but poor Alex is sitting there, bewildered, not knowing WHAT'S going on, and all you want to do is smash some test tubes, tell everyone to shut up, and pull Alex out of class.

So you guess you ARE his keeper, in a way.

At least that's how you feel.

Someone has to be.

Lunchroom

You're dining alone today.

Partly because you have to, partly because you choose to.

You HAVE to because Alex has split. You didn't see him go, but he hasn't been in school ever since chem.

You CHOOSE to because the alternative is sitting with Jay, and at this moment you'd rather have lunch with a rabid weasel.

You weren't feeling this way a few minutes ago. But then Jay made his appearance on the lunch line behind you.

"Duckomatic," he said. "The Duckmeister! Duckington! Duckter Dolittle!"

(When oh WHEN will he grow out of this habit?)

You nodded and forced a smile.

"What's the matter?" Jay said loudly. "You're not TALKING to me anymore?"

"When you give me a chance, I am," you replied.

"Why?"

"Maybe I should cut classes and wear dirty clothes and pull away from all my friends. And, like, slink along the hallway walls?"

"What are you talking about?"

"You know, I'll be like Snyder. THEN you'll hang with old Jay."

All of this delivered with a big, dumb, Cro Mag smile.

"I don't believe you're saying this," you said. "He happens to be my friend. And yeah, I hang with him,

BUT YOU KNOW WHY. YOU KNOW HE'S HAVING SOME ROUGH TIMES."

"RIGHT, RIGHT.... HEY, DO THEY HAVE CHOCOLATE PUDDING TODAY?"

"HE WAS YOUR FRIEND TOO."

"OK, OK. LIGHTEN UP, MCDUCK. CAN'T YOU TAKE A JOKE?"

"I GUESS I DIDN'T FIND IT FUNNY."

"I GUESS NOT. LOOKS LIKE HE'S RUBBING OFF ON YOU TOO."

YOU DIDN'T HONOR THAT ONE. YOU TOOK YOUR TRAY AND WALKED TO THE OPPOSITE SIDE OF THE CAFETERIA.

JAY'S WITH THE CRO MAGS NOW. EATING AND GRUNTING AND LAUGHING AND FARTING AND LOVING IT. LIVING PROOF THAT NOT ALL HUMAN LIFE IS AT THE TOP OF THE EVOLUTIONARY LADDER.

YOU'VE TOTALLY LOST YOUR APPETITE. YOU'RE WORRIED ABOUT ALEX, FOR ONE THING. AND EVEN THOUGH YOU KNOW YOU SHOULDN'T TAKE A WORD OF JAY'S SERIOUSLY, YOU FEEL GUILTY.

ARE YOU SPENDING TOO MUCH TIME WITH ALEX?

ARE YOU IGNORING JAY BECAUSE OF HIM?

NOT THAT THERE AREN'T MANY REASONS TO IGNORE A GUY WHO SETS YOU UP ON BLIND DATES WITHOUT EVEN ASKING, WHO HANGS WITH CRO MAGS, OBSESSES OVER GIRLS, AND PLAYS ON SO MANY AFTER-SCHOOL SPORTS TEAMS THAT YOU COULDN'T HAVE A FRIENDSHIP EVEN IF YOU WANTED TO.

So don't sweat it, Ducky.

You have other friends now — Sunny and Dawn and Maggie and Amalia. OK, they're only 13 and they're not guys. But they're smart and funny and they care about you — appreciate who you REALLY are, whoever that is — and they don't try to make you into a carbon copy of themselves, the way Jay does.

THAT'S why you're not close to Jay.

Enough said.

Case closed.

Math book opened.

Study begun.

After math:

The aftermath

The studying didn't help.

End of Study Hall
End of Patience

You called Alex's house from a pay phone after lunch. No answer.

Now, at the beginning of study hall, you ask the teacher for a library pass and then bypass the library (they never check) to look for Alex in all the usual places. And some of the unusual ones too. Behind the sports equipment shed. Off campus, at the Fiesta Grill.

You find Sunny at the Fiesta. She is sipping a fruit drink and reading a magazine. She greets you with a scream of joy and a big hug. You notice the edge of a terry cloth beach towel sticking out of her backpack.

"Hanging ten with the pound masters today?" you ask.

Sunny gives you her best MOI? look. "But enough about me. Sit. Have some papaya shake. Tell me what's wrong — and don't say 'Nothing,' Ducky. I know that look on your face."

How can you resist her? You can't.

So you tell her everything on your mind. All your concerns about Alex.

Her response? "I cut classes. I skip school. And you don't worry about ME like that."

"I worry about you all the time!"

"Then I guess Alex and I are BOTH lucky!" Sunny says with a big laugh. "Look, you want my advice? Venice Beach."

"Sunny —"

"I'm serious. Depressed people NEED sunshine. It does something chemical to the brain. That's a medical fact."

"Thank you, Doctor."

Sunny holds out her hand. "That'll be seventy-five dollars."

You laugh. You leave. You feel MUCH better.

Which is weird. You KNOW she's cutting. You KNOW she's heading for the beach. And you know that, in a way, she's just as messed up as Alex.

But Sunny's problems are different.

Not EASIER. But more concrete. More understandable.

You KNOW why she's angry. You KNOW why she does the things she does — cuts school, runs away, latches onto Perfect Guys who turn out to be jerks.

All of it is tied to her mom's condition. And as HORRIBLE and MORBID and PESSIMISTIC as it sounds, you know the cause of the problems will end someday.

But when you try to understand Alex, it's not so clear. What's the CAUSE? The Snyders' divorce? Maybe, but that's old news. And he insists he's over it.

So what else?

You wish there were something else you could point to and say, Once THIS is over with, he'll feel a lot better.

Maybe there just isn't.

Maybe there is, and Alex is hiding it.

If only he'd talk.

If only he'd show a little emotion.

Rage.

SOMETHING.

Home Alone
Ted at School; Mom and Dad Sleeping

You can't concentrate for the rest of the day. You are especially pathetic in Shakespeare, your favorite class with your favorite teacher — you can't answer ONE question about Measure for Measure even though you READ it and LIKED it, and you feel like a jerk for letting Ms. Krueger (and yourself) down.

So you decide to pop in to see her after school.

"Hi," you say. "Sorry about today."

Ms. Krueger smiles. She says you're sweet to come and apologize, but not to worry, we all have our off days.

You discuss the play a little, and just as you're about to leave, she reaches for the pile of today's assignment sheets and asks, "Will you be seeing Alex this evening? I'd like him to read one of these."

You tell her you'll give it to him, and you take the sheet.

"I haven't seen him for awhile. Is he sick?" Ms. K asks.

"Well, not really. I mean, not _physically_."

She shoots you a silent question mark.

A calm, kind, open, understanding, nonjudgmental question mark.

And you think about the time those kids trashed her house when she was on vacation. You remember how fair and patient her reaction was. And you've seen how NICE she is to Alex, despite the fact that he cuts her class so often.

You don't want to go behind Alex's back, but you feel you should tell her SOMETHING:

D: "The way he is right now? He's not really like that."

Ms. K [quietly shutting the classroom door]: "You know, Ducky, your friend is a very bright guy...."

D: "...but he's in serious danger of failing tenth grade. I know. He used to be a good student, Ms. Krueger. All A's and B's."

Ms. K: "I was impressed with his writing earlier in the year. Very powerful stuff — but disturbing. Bleak. I tried to talk to him about it, but it was difficult."

D: "He's totally depressed. He sleeps all the time. He doesn't care about the way he looks. I try to make him SEE how he's changing. I try to help him, but I can't get through."

Ms. K: "Maybe he should see the school psychologist."

D: "I guess." [You don't have the heart to tell her about Dr. Welsch and all the OTHER therapists who are history.] "But I should be able to do something too. I'm his best friend. What would YOU do if you were me?"

Ms. K [thinking for a moment]: "Everything you ARE doing, plus one more very big thing."

D: "What's that?"

Ms. K: "Never, ever, ever give up. You can't solve his problems, and you mustn't lose yourself trying. But you can let him know he's VALUED. And keep it up, even if it seems he doesn't appreciate it.

Something you say or do may be the thing that helps him regain his own perspective. When he eventually comes around, he'll never forget it. And neither will you."

You nod. You thank her.

You leave before she can see you starting to cry.

Not that she's solved anything.

Not that she's told you anything you didn't know, really.

But it feels so good to TALK about it.

On your way out, you see Maggie, Amalia, and Dawn, all huddled together in the front hall. Amalia's in the middle, scribbling something into a sketch pad.

They gesture you over.

There are three different designs for the name VANISH on the pad.

"We're designing a new logo," Amalia explains. "Which one looks right for a group?"

You stare at the logos.

VANISH

VANISH

VANISH

You try to make a decision, but you can't.

They all look the same.

Somehow, all you can think about is Alex's face.

In which Ducky, on the Bench at Cosmo's Gas Station, Seeks His Muse

After that last entry, you put away your journal and bike over to Alex's.

Mrs. Snyder answers the bell. She's smoking a cigarette. As usual.

You're scared. As usual. Even though it's SILLY to be scared of her — you're bigger than she is now and she's always perfectly nice to you — it's just a feeling left over from when you were a kid, when you hated the way she yelled all the time and you wondered how a nice guy like Alex could have such a MEAN mother.

But she's not mean, you KNOW that — she's a good mom and she works hard. She's just not a JOLLY person, and you wouldn't be either if you went through a bad divorce and had to work two jobs to support a family.

So you smile and politely ask about Alex, but she looks confused. She says he's out. She thought he was with YOU.

You say you haven't seen him (you're about to add the words "since chemistry class" but you swallow them).

"Well, your guess is as good as mine, Ducky," she

says. "If you see him, tell him to leave me a note once in awhile."

She takes a deep drag from her cigarette. Her eyes are red and she's pulling a loose lock of hair behind her ear.

And you wonder, Does she know what's going on? She must. SOMEONE has been paying for the therapy and the antidepression medication. Alex's dad sure isn't.

"Mrs. Snyder..." You want to say something but you don't know what. You can't talk about Alex behind his back, but you want to reassure her somehow — she looks like she needs reassurance. But all you can say is, "I'm sure he's at the park," and you go.

You're right. Alex is in the park. Exactly where you expect him to be. You cross the bridge and find him at the other side, sitting on the creek bank among the reeds.

You call out to him.

He grunts hello. He doesn't look up.

You park your bike and sit next to him. "What's up?"

No answer. He's ripping up grass, one blade at a time.

You pull out a long blade, make a reed between

your THUMBS, AND BLOW. IT MAKES A GOOD, SOLID SCREEEEK, AND A DUCK FLAPS ITS WINGS IN SURPRISE.

The Old Alex would have tried to outdo you.

The new one is not interested. His face is a total blank. As if the muscles have been cut loose, leaving the skin to slacken.

So you shut up. Listen to the breeze. Skim stones on the water. And you think about the long summer afternoons you two used to spend here, doing nothing, absolutely nothing, exactly as you're doing now.

Except back then, time passed so quickly. You talked about the same things over and over, or you spent hours playing the ESP game, and it was never boring.

"Tell me — right this minute," you blurt out. "What song are you hearing in your head?"

You hope for a match. Just like old times.

But Alex yawns. "No music."

You fling a perfect, flat stone and it skitters across the creek — all the way to the other bank. "Yesss!" you cry out.

No reaction.

"Alex," you finally say, "are you OK?"

He nods. "Uh-huh."

"You seem ... I don't know, upset?"

Shrug.

"Is something going on? Something you want to talk about?"

The words sound so weak, so wimpy. But you're trying, you're NOT GIVING UP.

Alex keeps his eyes straight ahead. He looks as if he's thinking about what to say, shaping an answer.

But he just yawns. "You wouldn't understand."

Slap.

What now, Ducky?

You're thinking: FINE, he wants to be that way? He wants to abuse his best friend? He can stay here alone.

See if the reeds understand. See if the birds understand.

You get up, ready to leave, but you catch yourself.

You look closely at his face.

He's not dissing you. He's telling you the truth. HIS truth.

He honestly believes you wouldn't understand.

And maybe he's right. You've never had the URGE to do the things he does — drink or cut school or mope around and do nothing. It's not in your chemistry.

Step 1 to helping somebody with a problem is sympathy, and how can you sympathize with someone so different, someone whose mind used to be just like yours but has now veered off into the Twilight Zone?

No matter what you say or do — stay, leave, turn cartwheels, throw yourself in the creek — the blank expression won't change. You don't mean anything to him. Nothing does.

Never, ever, ever give up. You repeat that to yourself, even though it sounds about as possible as Flap your arms and fly.

You sit next to him. Silently.

He doesn't move.

You want him to know what you and Ms. Krueger talked about, that he might fail tenth grade. You want to tell him that his teachers are concerned. But you can't bring yourself to say it.

Maybe later. Maybe if he snaps out of whatever he's in.

If he opens up just a little.

You sit for a long time, quietly watching the sun set, until you realize you're starving, and you convince Alex to ride home with you.

Mrs. Snyder is at the door when you arrive. You can hear her scolding him as he walks in, but even from the sidewalk you can see the relief on her face.

Afterward, you're exhausted and your brain is overflowing with thoughts. You don't want to go home, not just yet.

So you stop off here, at Cosmo's.

And you write.

Which makes you feel a little better.

Very little.

BUT IT SURE WAS BETTER THAN YOU FEEL RIGHT NOW!

What a jerk.

Cosmo's?

What were you thinking?

You just sat there, scribbling away, not even looking at the time.

Wake up, McCrae. It's not The Ducky and Ted Show anymore. You're a family again.

And your family eats dinner at 6:00. Always has.

So when you walked in at 7:15, and Dad was standing in the kitchen doorway, tapping his foot and looking at his watch, WHAT DID YOU EXPECT?

Way to go. Ruin everything. After Mom and Dad had planned a special "family reunion celebration" — vegetarian lasagna, sparkling cider, ice-cream sundaes — your favorite dishes, made especially for you.

AND YOU WERE AT COSMO'S.

Yes, they're jet-lagged. Yes, they were eating lunch during your breakfast, and they were asleep when you got home from school. It didn't occur to you that life would slip back into a normal routine so soon. But you could have called. You didn't have to act as if they were still in Ghana.

And then — then, when Dad yelled at you, did you apologize? No, you made excuses. You told them Ted and you NEVER eat precisely at 6. You eat when you're hungry — 7:30, 9:00, midnight, whenever.

Which is NOT what they wanted to hear and just made the atmosphere worse.

So even though you WEREN'T hungry, you sat in the kitchen and ate leftovers while everyone else cleaned up, and Ted glared at you the whole time as if to say HOW'D I GET STUCK WITH THE DISHES? which was ridiculous because you would trade places with him in a minute.

After the cleanup, Mom and Dad sat with you while you finished eating. You apologized and they accepted it. But you could see they were hurt, and you felt awful. Dad suggested another celebration tomorrow — this time at 8:15, after you finish work at Winslow Books. You agreed and then actually TRIED to start a conversation, to begin catching up on all the

MONTHS THEY WERE AWAY, BUT THE PHONE BEGAN RINGING FOR THEM, AND IT HASN'T STOPPED.

Anyway, you're back in your room again. It's a chilly night but you can't turn on the heat the way you normally would, because the thermostat reads 61° and Dad won't let you "waste electricity" unless it's under 60.

You feel as if you're 10 years old and you've been sent to your room for bad behavior.

Oh, well, look on the bright side.

For almost 24 hours, you've had something you were looking forward to — a REAL FAMILY again.

Cherish those 24 hours. Value them.

You took care of Mom and Dad at the airport. You took care of your ailing friend.

You also alienated your parents. And you alienated your friend.

Oh. And you probably flunked your math test.

Guess you're batting a thousand, Ducky.

Thursday 12/3
Lunch & Loose Ends

You meant to stop by Alex's on the way to school, but you didn't.

WHY?

Because you were lazy. Tired. You wanted a break from the INTENSITY. Whatever.

But Alex didn't show up at school. Hasn't been here all day long.

You should have dragged him to school, the way you did yesterday.

You GAVE UP, Ducky. You're not supposed to do that, remember?

Now what?

DO something, that's what.

35 more minutes until the end of lunch.

Maybe I can find him.

Maybe I should cut school myself.

South of Psychology
East of Self-Help

The sections, that is.

You're working tonight. At Winslow Books.

You figure if you stand here long enough, the vibes from the books will teach you something.

Anyway, it's break time. You have fifteen minutes. So write fast.

Since we last spoke:

1. You didn't cut. You chickened out.
2. You didn't find Alex either. You called his house from a pay phone at school, but no one answered.
3. You had some long-overdue face time with Sunny.

Number 3 happened after school. You were freaking out because you wanted to stop by Alex's but you only had twenty minutes to report to Winslow Books.

Then you heard Sunny call out, "You're giving me a ride."

Not a question. A command.

(You have to love her. She is so cool.)

You said, "My rates have gone up," but she ignored you and climbed into the passenger seat.

"Winslow Books, please, servant."

"What's the occasion?" you asked, driving away. "Your dad hired you for the Christmas rush?"

"What, and scare away the customers? Nope. He's taking me to visit Dorian."

"Dorian?"

"As in The Picture of Dorian Gray? The picture that ages before your eyes?"

"Are you talking about your MOM?"

"She calls HERSELF that. You have to admit, Ducky, she does look about 100 years old."

You bit your tongue. Sometimes you can't believe what comes out of Sunny's mouth.

But that's SUNNY, that's her style. Keep everyone off guard, break down their barriers. Laugh in the face of your troubles. Use extreme humor, if you have to — whatever keeps you going.

You admire that, kind of. But right then you didn't know how to respond. You were thinking there was something strange going on. Sunny almost always goes to the hospital alone — SOMETIMES with a trusted friend, but NEVER with her dad unless it's an emergency.

"Mom's MUCH worse," Sunny explained. "It's just a matter of months, I guess. Maybe weeks. Some Christmas present, huh?" She popped a stick of gum in her mouth and held the pack out to you. "Want some?"

Sunny was trying to be cool, but her face and body were giving her away. She was coiled up, intense. Her eyes were slitted and anxious.

You could tell she was scared out of her wits.

"I could go with you," you volunteered.

Sunny laughed. "Right. Dad's probably already calculating how much business he'll lose by leaving the store. Don't be surprised if he CHAINS you to the cash register."

You pulled into the store's parking lot. You expected Sunny to jump right out, but she didn't. She was looking down at the floor, gripping the dashboard.

You put your hand over hers. "Good luck," you said.

She whirled around, threw her arms around you, and gave you a kiss on the cheek. Then, without a word, she left the car.

You caught up to her. Mr. Winslow was waiting by the front door, pacing, looking at his watch. He started barking out instructions to you — clean up the spill in the children's book section, open the two UPS boxes, find another shelf for New Age books, make

SURE TO OBEY THE STORE MANAGER WHILE HE'S GONE, ETC.,
ETC., ETC.

YOU WATCHED HIM AND SUNNY WALK AWAY TO HIS CAR.

YOU WISHED THERE WAS SOMETHING YOU COULD DO, SOME
WAY YOU COULD MAKE IT ALL BETTER.

BUT YOU KNEW THERE WASN'T.

IT SEEMS THERE NEVER IS.

SIIILENT NIIIIGHT...

YOU'RE BEAT. YOU CAN BARELY HOLD A PEN AND IT'S
BEDTIME. BUT YOUR MIND IS ZINGY, SO HERE GOES.

YOU WORKED AT THE STORE NONSTOP. VERY BUSY.

YOU DIDN'T NOTICE MR. WINSLOW COME BACK AROUND
7:15, BECAUSE HE WAS SO QUIET. WHICH WAS TOTALLY WEIRD,
BECAUSE HE'S ALWAYS YELLING ABOUT SOMETHING.

TONIGHT HE WAS IN ANOTHER WORLD, WANDERING,
RESHELVING BOOKS, READING. SUNNY WASN'T WITH HIM; HE'D
TAKEN HER HOME.

YOU FINALLY WORKED UP THE COURAGE TO ASK ABOUT HIS
WIFE. HE LOOKED AT YOU — REALLY LOOKED YOU IN THE EYE
FOR THE FIRST TIME SINCE HE HIRED YOU — AND SAID IN A
SOFT VOICE, "YOU'RE KIND TO ASK, CHRIS."

PERIOD.

Nothing else.

Which just made you worry more.

At 8:00 you left and made SURE to be home for Family Dinner: The Sequel. It was hard to concentrate. You were thinking about Mrs. Winslow and whether or not you should call Sunny.

Dad made a pretty good homemade pizza, and Mom passed around some just-developed photos that actually made the Ghana trip look like a GOOD TIME. Soon you were all laughing and chatting, and it felt OK, like the old days, sort of. Ye Older Son Ted gave a boring yet corny toast, and Dad requested that we all have "a little McCrae bonding time" on Saturday, "maybe a special trip or something."

Cool. Good idea.

You kind of wish YOU had thought of a toast too. But you had a lot on your mind.

After dessert, when Mom, Dad, and Ted went into the den to watch the tube, YOU went to the phone to call Sunny's house, then Alex's.

No answer at either place.

You left a message on their machines, asking them to call back.

It's now 10:47. Neither called.

It's probably too late to call again.

Mrs. Snyder and Paula are probably asleep. Mr.
Winslow too.

Chill, Ducky.

Try again tomorrow.

TOMORROW
Also Known as Friday

You call Alex. He's home. And the conversation
goes like this:

D: "What's up?"

A: "Whatever."

D: "Everything OK?"

A: "I guess."

D: "Coming to school?"

A: "I have to."

D: "I'll take you."

A: "Mom's driving me."

D: "Cool."

That's what you love about talking to Alex. The
repartee. The crackling wit.

Oh, well. At least he's not skipping school.

In Which Ducky Sees
a Light at the End of the Tunnel

Very faint. A SUGGESTION of a light.

You spot Alex after homeroom. He's walking down the hallway slowly, slumped over, his shoulder practically pressed against the wall, his hair hanging down over his face.

The usual.

You catch up. Say hi. Talk a little.

Then, as you're about to part ways — here it comes, drumroll, please — he says, "What are you doing after school?"

"Nothing," you say. "You?"

He shrugs. "I don't know. Want to hang?"

"Sure."

Ta-da.

You never thought a question like that would MAKE YOUR DAY.

But it does.

You Have Seen the Mountaintop
and It Looks Like the Pits

After school you wait for Alex by his locker. You haven't seen him since lunch.

Miracle of miracles, he comes shuffling along. Still in school after a FULL DAY.

You call out to him. "So, where do you want to go?"

He looks a little confused.

"To hang out?" you remind him.

"I don't know, drive around, I guess," he says. "The park."

"Cool beans." You pack up your books. Alex isn't even bothering to touch his locker.

"No homework?" you ask.

"No."

OK. Fine.

You walk out together.

The moment you get through the door, you hear a loud quacking sound, followed by, "It's the Duckster!"

You turn to see Jay grinning at you. His arm is around Lisa Bergonzi. Marco Bardwell and Mad Moose Machover are there too. They're both snickering and communicating with each other with some prehistoric Cro Mag mutterings.

You say hi and turn away.

"Hold it!" Jay's running toward you now, looking all excited about something. "Hey, Duckboy, you remember LeeAnn?"

At the sound of Jay's voice, you see Alex's face tense.

You are NOT thrilled, because the name LEEANN brings back a certain horrifying BLIND DOUBLE DATE you would much, much rather forget.

"I know, I know, I shouldn't have set you up with her, OK?" Jay says. "But listen. She has this cousin, she's visiting from Sweden for a week during Christmas vacation — SWEDEN, Duckington — and she's just like you, sort of shy and smart, and she doesn't have a boyfriend —"

"I don't believe you're telling me this," you say.

"Why? I'm letting you know in advance!"

"I DON'T LIKE BEING SET UP AT ALL, OK? Let Moose ask her out."

"Not my type," Moose mumbles.

"Not DUCKY's type either," Marco cracks, and they both start guffawing as if it were the funniest joke in the world.

"Alex?" Jay says hopefully. Like he's auctioning off the girl to the highest bidder.

"Huh?" Alex replies.

Jay rolls his eyes. "Forget it." With a big sigh he swaggers back to his group.

"Ducky and Alex are happy just as they are," Moose says.

The laughter creeps under your skin as you walk toward the parking lot.

"I used to like Jay," Alex mutters.

"He can be OK." You don't know WHY ON EARTH you're defending Jay.

You get in the car and cruise away from school. Alex is in a foul mood. Not numb, not spacey, just foul. His arms are folded and he's glaring straight ahead.

"Where do you want to go?" you ask.

"No place you can take me," he grumbles.

What does THAT mean?

You have no idea. You don't want to know.

You're driving toward Las Palmas County Park, but you know that Jay and his friends are likely to show up there, so you switch directions and head for the Alta Mira Hills.

As you approach the lot, Alex suddenly sits forward. "Let's go rock climbing," he says.

You're so stunned you nearly agree on the spot.

But you think of all the stuff you NEED for rock

CLIMBING, AND IF YOU HEAD HOME TO GET YOUR PITONS AND ROPES AND FRICTION SHOES, YOU'LL BE ANOTHER HALF HOUR CLOSER TO DARKNESS.

"IT'S KIND OF LATE," YOU SAY. "HOW ABOUT JUST A HIKE? WE CAN GO CLIMBING ON SUNDAY. MOM AND DAD ARE TAKING TED AND ME SOMEWHERE TOMORROW."

"WHATEVER," ALEX REPLIES.

THE ALTA MIRA LOT IS ALMOST EMPTY. YOU PARK NEAR THE TRAILHEAD, AND SOON YOU AND ALEX ARE HIKING UP THE HILL.

YOU GO SIDE BY SIDE, SILENTLY, UNTIL THE PATH NARROWS. THEN YOU PULL AHEAD.

FAR AHEAD. SO WHEN HE CRIES OUT, "DUCKY!" YOU CAN'T SEE HIM.

YOU RACE DOWN, NEARLY TRIPPING OVER A ROOT.

HE'S STANDING IN THE MIDDLE OF THE PATH, POINTING INTO THE WOODS.

A COYOTE IS LOPING AMONG THE BUSHES, SNIFFING AND POKING ITS SNOUT BETWEEN THE ROCKS.

THE TRACE OF A SMILE FLICKERS ACROSS ALEX'S FACE. "AN EARTHLING," HE SAYS.

YOU CAN'T BELIEVE THIS. HE REMEMBERS. IT'S EXACTLY THE KIND OF STUPID THING YOU USED TO SAY AS SIRHC AND XELA, ALIEN LIFE-FORMS ON THEIR EVER-RECURRING SEARCH FOR SIGNS OF HUMAN LIFE.

(YOU WERE NERDS, DUCKY!)

Now the coyote is walking away with a Snickers wrapper in its mouth. "See how tenderly it cares for its young?" you say.

Alex lets out a little laughlike exhalation through his nose, and you realize this is the CLOSEST he's come to expressing an EMOTION in ages.

You realize the good mood may not last long. This may be an opening.

D: "Alex?"

A: "Yeah?"

D: "So. Feeling better today?"

A: "Better than what?"

D [deep breath]: "You seem different. In a GOOD way, I mean. More like YOU."

A: "I'm always me."

He starts hiking away. You follow.

D: "You know what I mean. The YOU before — all the stuff happened. The stuff that made you have to go to Dr. Welsch."

A: "People change."

D: "Alex, just out of curiosity — what do you DO when you stay home from school?"

A: "Sleep."

D: "Don't you sleep enough at night?"

A: "I guess not."

D: "Because if you did, you would go to school more often."

A: "Why should you care about that?"

D: "Why shouldn't I?"

A: "No one else does."

D: "Not true. Ms. Krueger does." [Cringe, shrink, melt — really, REALLY dumb, Ducky.] "I mean A LOT of people probably do."

A [turns to look at you]: "Like who? Who else besides you and Ms. Krueger?"

D: "Your friends. Your teachers. PROBABLY. I mean, it's a big deal. You could be left back — not that you WOULD, but I wouldn't be too happy about that —"

A [holding up his hand]: "Stop, OK? Stop lecturing me."

D: "I'm sorry. I don't mean to —"

A: "EVERYBODY lectures me, Ducky. I don't need you to join in."

D: "I'm just trying to be a FRIEND, that's all —"

A: "Friends leave you alone. I thought YOU were a friend. You were the only one who let me be, Ducky. Up until now."

D: "OK. OK. I'll stop."

Alex walks away. You follow.

And you feel like a total wimp.

Sleep.

That's what Alex does when he's cutting school.

HOW CAN A PERSON SLEEP SO MUCH?

Does he NEED it? Does he have some kind of weird sleep disorder? Is THAT the problem? Maybe he can't help staying home from school.

So go ahead and open your big mouth, Ducky. Tell him how to lead his life. Like you know everything.

He was just starting to feel better. You could see it.

And you set him back.

NICE.

WORK.

11:47 P.M.

You're nuts.

Alex doesn't have a sleep disorder.

YOU'RE the one with the sleep disorder.

Your mind is so full of nonsense that you can't think straight.

You did not say TOO MUCH.

The truth is, you didn't say ENOUGH.

He WANTS you to be silent, he LIKES it because it doesn't CHALLENGE him, it lets him think: Hey, it's ALL RIGHT to cut school and flunk out because DUCKY doesn't mind, HE doesn't think it's so bad, and he's my BEST FRIEND.

What you did was the OPPOSITE of friendship. You backed down. You apologized. You promised to keep all this to yourself.

You were afraid to get him angry. You were afraid to let him yell and scream. Maybe he NEEDS to be shaken a little, by someone he TRUSTS. Someone who's not an authority figure.

You let him stay right where he was. In a rut.

THAT'S what you did wrong.

12:58 A.M.

But he's shaky. Unstable. If you yelled at him TOO much, maybe you would push him over the edge.

1:14

What's the difference?

Either way, you messed up.

You always mess up. You always choose the wrong thing to do.

THAT's what they'll call the movie of your life: <u>DO THE WRONG THING</u>.

Something A.M.

WHY CAN'T I SLEEP?

You know why you can't sleep.

You're an idiot.

You think you can handle this on your own.

You can't.

TALK TO SOMEONE. MOM AND DAD.

No. THEY WOULDN'T BE ANY HELP.

OR TED.

UH, RIGHT.

SUNNY? SHE HAS ENOUGH PROBLEMS.

MAGGIE'S BUSY ALL THE TIME.

JAY? HA-HA.

MAYBE DAWN OR AMALIA. BUT THEY HARDLY KNOW
ALEX. THEY DON'T NEED TO HEAR ALL THIS.

GUESS WHAT?

YOU'RE ALL ALONE ON THIS ONE, DUCKY BOY.

NO ONE TO TALK TO.

JUST LIKE ALEX.

NO, NOT REALLY.

ALEX HAS YOU.

BUT YOU DON'T HAVE ALEX.

Greetings
from the State of
Disbelief

You can barely open your eyes. The sun is killing you.

But you have to wash up, eat breakfast, and get dressed.

Your family outing is about to begin.

To Disneyland.

They have GOT to be kidding.

In the Car

Don't know how long you'll be able to write. Dad's driving and you forgot to bring Dramamine.

When you were TWO, you loved Disneyland. SIX. Even TEN. You must have gone there about 7,000 times before you hit your teens.

It's not that you HATE the place. You don't.

But it's OLD now.

YOU'RE old.

You tried to give them a hint. Subtle little facial

CLUES. BODY LANGUAGE. FINALLY YOU JUST SAID, "MOM, WE'RE
NOT KIDS ANYMORE."

"OF COURSE NOT," MOM SAID PLEASANTLY. "WE
WOULDN'T LEAVE KIDS HOME ALONE WHILE WE WERE IN
GHANA."

TED CALLED YOU AN OLD FART. HE LOVES THE IDEA.

DAD SAID, "COME ON, DUCKY. FOR OLD TIMES' SAKE."

THEN YOU KNEW. IT'S SOME KIND OF RETRO IRONIC
NOSTALGIA THING.

YOU CAN UNDERSTAND THAT. SORT OF.

OK, ATTITUDE ADJUSTMENT, McCRAE.

YOU CAN DO IT.

YIPPEE.

MAIN STREET, U.S.A.
IN LINE FOR "GREAT MOMENTS WITH MR. LINCOLN"

TED WAS THE ONE WHO SUGGESTED THIS.

HE'S REGRESSING.

SO'S DAD. WHEN WE PASSED THE OLD FIRE ENGINE, HE
CALLED OUT, "DUCKY! FAH-OH TUCK!" LIKE YOU'D FIND IT SO
CUTE TO BE REMINDED OF WHAT YOU SAID AS A CHILD, IN
FRONT OF FIVE DOZEN TOURISTS WHO ARE PROBABLY

WONDERING WHAT TWO GROWN SONS ARE DOING IN DISNEYLAND WITH THEIR PARENTS.

YOU SMILED AND WALKED AWAY. YOU SENT HIM A TELEPATHIC ANTI-HUMILIATION WARNING.

YOU FORGOT TO SEND THEM TO TED. SOON YOU WERE WATCHING THE BARBERSHOP QUARTET AND HE BEGAN SINGING ALONG. LOUD.

WHILE YOU BACKED AWAY IN HORROR, DAD EGGED HIM ON AND MOM PULLED OUT HER VIDEOCAMERA TO RECORD HIM — ALL THE WHILE TELLING EVERYONE IN EARSHOT ABOUT HIS UPCOMING SHOW IN COLLEGE.

ENDURE, DUCKY. ENDURE. ABE LINCOLN HAD IT WORSE AT YOUR AGE.

HE'S ABOUT TO TELL YOU HOW.

FOR THE HUNDREDTH TIME.

WAITING OUTSIDE
THE ENCHANTED TIKI ROOM

ANOTHER LINE.

SCREAMING, SQUIRMING KIDS.

NOW DAD IS PULLING PING-PONG BALLS OUT OF HIS POCKET. TO DO MAGIC TRICKS.

WHY?

WHY?

WHY?

In Which Ducky Eats Humble Pie

OK, you have to admit it.

He isn't bad.

No David Copperfield, but not bad.

The kids loved him. They asked for autographs. Their parents took pictures.

Then he gave you the Ping-Pong balls. So YOU started doing tricks. The way he taught you. What else could you do?

Hey, it made the wait easier. Always did, even when you were a kid.

The Enchanted Tiki Room was an anticlimax.

Maybe they should put some feathers on Dad and make him part of the act.

The Tale of Wild Woman Mom
(Written Aboard the Disney Railroad)

She's brave. She's smart. She remembers what EVERYONE likes, and she won't waver in her path to each ride in the right order. "No, Herb. Ducky hates that ride. We have to go to Frontierland.... Ted has to see the sailing ship.... Save your appetites for the Blue Ribbon Bakery, guys!"

Not only that, folks, she remembers EVERY event from EVERY family trip. She'll tell you things you've forgotten:

→ You once threw a tantrum in the penny arcade.
→ A Pluto-teer (or whatever they call those people in Pluto costumes) scared you so badly you shrieked until you fell asleep in your stroller from exhaustion.
→ You used to have nightmares about the Pirates of the Caribbean, and for months afterward, anyone with an eye patch made you cry.

When you mention Haunted Mansion, she says, "Ducky, are you SURE you want to go in there?" As if you're STILL scared of it.

Ted's teasing her.

That's OK. Mom's cool. She can take it.

She's got his barbershop quartet singing debut on
tape.

Blackmail is the best revenge.

Frontierland
Tom Sawyer Island

The caves have gotten so much smaller.

So have the keelboats.

And you can't actually steer them with poles.

Didn't you used to be able to do that?

Or did you just imagine it? The way you imagined
you were Davy Crockett and Alex was Mike Fink,
battling it out on the river?

Or did Alex play Davy while you were Mike?

Whatever.

C U REAL SOON!
Y? BECAUSE WE LIKE U...

AND SO, THE McCRAES DEPART THE KINGDOM, BELLIES FULL, SMILES ON THEIR FACES.

HOW WAS IT?

WEIRD. FUN.

WRONG. RIGHT.

TED'S HAPPY. HE MET A GIRL AND GOT HER PHONE NUMBER.

MOM AND DAD LEFT THE PARK HOLDING HANDS AND SMILING.

YOU DIDN'T MIND IT, OVERALL.

TOMORROWLAND WAS A LITTLE TOUGH. THAT WAS ALEX'S FAVE. ESPECIALLY SPACE MOUNTAIN. YOU FELT A LITTLE GUILTY THAT YOU DIDN'T ASK HIM TO COME ALONG.

BUT DON'T KID YOURSELF.

HE WOULD HAVE SAID NO.

BESIDES, THIS WAS A FAMILY OUTING.

YOU NEED THEM ONCE IN AWHILE.

Sunday
Writing Fast

In Alex's room. Alone.

He's in the shower.

He was supposed to be ready for rock climbing by 9:30. You got here on time. But Mrs. S told you he was asleep. "You go wake him. I can't."

You climbed up here. You knocked and opened the door.

The smell hit you first. Musty, stuffy, like he hadn't opened a window in ages.

You couldn't believe your eyes.

Piles of clothes. Scattered papers. Magazines. Empty cups & dishes.

Pigsty.

Worse than Ted.

Alex was never NEAT, but he NEVER used to let things get this bad.

You woke him up. He seemed surprised to see you. Then he apologized and slouched into the bathroom to get ready.

You felt sorry for him, so you started to clean up.

No big deal. A little pile management. Floor liberation.

A JEANS JACKET WAS ON THE FLOOR, SCRUNCHED BY THE FOOT OF THE BED, SO YOU PICKED IT UP.

AND A BOTTLE FELL OUT.

A FIFTH OF VODKA. HALF EMPTY.

YOU BENT DOWN TO PICK IT UP.

AND YOU SAW ANOTHER ONE — TOTALLY EMPTY — UNDER HIS BED.

YOU PUT THE JACKET BACK. WITH THE BOTTLE.

NOW WHAT?

YOU ARE FREAKED.

SHOULD YOU TELL HIM?

EVEN THOUGH HE WANTS YOU TO LAY OFF?

WHAT SHOULD YOU

Alex, Part 2
At the Monfort Quarry
Between a Rock and a Hard Place

BACK AGAIN.

HAD TO STOP WRITING, BECAUSE YOU HEARD THE SHOWER TURNING OFF.

YOU'RE ALONE HERE FOR A FEW MINUTES. ALEX IS OFF TO THE CONVENIENCE MART TO GET SOME SPORTS DRINK AND TRAIL GORP.

You hope that's ALL he's getting....

You didn't write that.

BAD thing to say, Ducky, about your best friend. BUT YOU CAN'T HELP IT. How can you trust him now?

You try to be close, you open yourself up, you let him confide in you. You ask him what's wrong — YOU GIVE HIM EVERY CHANCE TO TELL THE TRUTH. And he tells you nothing's wrong, nothing CONCRETE, it's depression, he's dealing with it — when all along, that's NOT it at all.

He has a drinking problem.

And all you can think is, WHY DIDN'T I GUESS THIS? The slurry speech, the tiredness, the depression — it makes sense, because alcohol is a DEPRESSANT, isn't it?

Then he walks into the room, his hair still wet from the shower, and you're sitting on the bed, arms folded like a guilty little kid who's done something wrong.

He's groggy. Yawning. He looks around the room.

"You cleaned up," he says.

"I'd forgotten what color the carpet is."

"You didn't have to clean up. Things will just fall back into a mess."

His eyes fix on the jeans jacket.

Out of the corner of your eye you see that the tip of the bottle is sticking out.

STUPID. You were too rushed, too careless.

"You found the bottles," he says.

But he sounds calm. Matter-of-fact.

You stammer and splutter.

"No big deal," he says. "I've always had them around. Haven't opened them for ages."

You don't believe him for a minute.

You didn't talk about it on the way here.

But you haven't stopped thinking.

Alex makes no sense. You don't know him anymore. You don't know what to expect.

The possibilities?

1. He WANTED you to find out. He knew that if you came to his house, he'd be asleep and you'd have to wake him up, and once you were in his room you'd see the bottles. It's his way of crying for help.

2. He didn't mean for you to see them. In fact, today's plan — the rock climbing — is to convince you he doesn't have a problem anymore. He wants to fool you into thinking he's getting better. Then you won't BOTHER him so much.

3. He is getting better. He HASN'T touched the bottles in a long time. And he wants to go rock climbing.
4. None of the above. Or parts of all.

OK, nothing you can do now. Except CLIMB.

Try to enjoy it. The way you used to. It's the only athletic thing you and Alex were ever good at.

Just make sure the ropes are secure and the pitons are tight.

And TRUST him.

You have to.

The rocks are pretty steep.

One false move, and you could be in serious trouble.

Sunday Night
Still Alive

Alex comes back from the convenience mart.

You load up the snacks and drinks. You double-check your Polaroid camera to make sure it has film.

And you start up the rock.

Right away you know this isn't going to be easy.

You're worried — not about yourself but about Alex.

You choose your handholds extra carefully. You jam your pitons extra securely. You make the first climb, while Alex waits. You call "On belay!" loud and clear. No room for error.

Then, when it's Alex's turn, you hold on for dear life.

His.

And yours.

One slip, and you bear all the weight. You're the only one keeping you both anchored to the earth.

You watch his every move. You try to anticipate every change in direction, every shift of weight.

Just like life.

Think about it: You're holding on for two, never letting up, whether Alex is moving or slipping or standing still. Knowing that whether or not he makes it depends on YOU.

The difference is, you reach a peak at the end of a climb. You rest.

You're bruised and aching and tired. But you feel great.

And your ropes are intact. Strong, not frayed.

You wish life were that simple.

Anyway, you make the climb. You scramble over the crest and help Alex pull himself up.

You're exhilarated. You feel INVINCIBLE.

Alex is taking off his gear. Looking back down the rock.

The smog has lifted, and the air is sweet and cool.

Time for a photo op.

You wedge your camera in the crook of a tree and set the self-timer.

"Quick!" You run to Alex and pose, your arm around his shoulder.

"No, Ducky —" Too late. The camera snaps.

As you run to see the picture, Alex sits on a flat rock and pulls his food from his pack.

You watch the image appear.

Next to your grinning, jack-o'-lantern face, Alex looks washed-out and ghostly. As if he's seeing something through the camera lens that you can't see. Something terrifying.

You pocket the photo and move to sit near him. He's staring out over the valley, the breeze sweeping back his hair.

He doesn't ask about the snapshot.

D [with a deep, satisfied sigh]: "Isn't it great?"

A: "As good as it gets. Which isn't too good."

D: "Hey, come on, we DID it. We're sitting at the top. THIS is what matters."

A: "Nothing matters."

D: "That's just not true, Alex. SO MUCH matters."

A: "Like what?"

D [this is hard]: "Like FRIENDS." [All 1 of them, who doesn't seem to be doing a great job.] "Family." [What's left of it.] "Simple stuff — the smell of the morning air through your bedroom window, the end of school on Friday, the beach on a weekend, a drive along the coast —"

A: "You're a hopeless optimist."

D: "I have my ups and downs. But I keep my eyes open. I let the good things in. What's wrong with that?"

A: "Whatever gets you through the night."

D: "What gets YOU through the night, Alex?"

A: "You don't want to know."

D: "What does THAT mean? Alex, look where we are. You wanted to do this. You suggested it! Are you so depressed you can't enjoy this? Is it like a tape running in your brain — 'No matter what, I WILL be gloomy'? Just turn it OFF for a moment. Let your senses take over. Look at the view, feel the breezes.

THIS IS IT, Alex. THIS IS LIFE. IF YOU CAN'T ENJOY THIS, WHAT'S THE POINT?"

A [NODS; THEN, SOFTLY, UNDER HIS BREATH]: "YUP. WHAT'S THE POINT?"

THAT HITS YOU HARD.

IT MAKES YOU THINK.

IT BRINGS UP THE UNANSWERED QUESTIONS HIDDEN AWAY IN THE BACK OF YOUR MIND SINCE Jay'S PARTY — WHY DID HE HIDE HIMSELF IN A LOCKED BATHROOM THAT NIGHT, AND WHY WAS HE FULLY CLOTHED IN THE TUB WITH THE SHOWER RUNNING?

EVEN BACK THEN YOU HAD A SUSPICION — YOU MUST HAVE, BECAUSE YOU DIDN'T WANT TO LET HIM OUT OF YOUR SIGHT, AND EVEN AFTER YOU LEFT, YOU WATCHED FROM OUTSIDE THE HOUSE UNTIL HIS BEDROOM LIGHT WAS OUT AND YOU WERE REASONABLY SURE HE'D GONE TO SLEEP.

AND NOW YOU HAVE TO FACE IT, AT THE ROCK SUMMIT WITH YOUR LIFELINES STILL TIED AND UNFRAYED. YOU HAVE TO ASK HIM.

YOU WAIT UNTIL YOU'RE BACK IN THE CAR, DRIVING DOWN THE FREEWAY WITH YOUR WINDOWS OPEN AND THE RADIO OFF.

D: "Alex, WHEN YOU SAY NOTHING MATTERS — YOU'RE NOT SPEAKING LITERALLY, RIGHT?"

A: "HUH?"

D: "Like, it doesn't mean you would want to stop living?"

A [snapping around to face you]: "No! What's with you, Ducky? You think just because there's no reason to live a person should want to kill himself?"

D: "No. I was speaking theoretically —"

A: "I mean, that's the LAST thing I would do!"

D: "OK, Alex. OK. You just said some stuff that concerned me —"

A: "I mean, just because there's no reason to LIVE, doesn't mean there's a reason to DIE!"

D: "Right. I won't mention it again."

A: "Don't even THINK about it."

Alex flicks on the radio.

You drive home to the Top 40 countdown.

Feeling much better.

How could you have asked him that, Ducky?

OK, you feel like you're attached to him. Like you have to pull the weight of two.

But cut the guy some slack.

You're on solid ground now.

Monday
Study Hall

He wasn't at his locker this morning. Not at lunch either.

After lunch you saw Ms. Krueger in the hallway. You turned and went to class the long way.

You couldn't face her. You knew she was going to ask how Alex is doing.

As if you have any idea.

And Now
a Word from Our Sponsor:
YOU.

Ducky.

The guy whose name is on the front of this journal. Whose life is supposed to be chronicled faithfully here.

Forgot about him, huh?

Forgot to mention you managed to pass the math test last week.

Congratulations. Thank you.

As usual, you're so wrapped up in Alex, you don't even think of yourself.

After school today, you give Amalia a ride home, and she's talking away, mentioning something about Maggie and her new therapist — and that makes you think about Dr. Welsch and your rock-climbing trip and the fact that Alex wasn't in school today, and as you pass the turnoff to his house, you start debating whether you should call him or pay a visit — and suddenly you notice the car is silent.

"Ducky, are you OK?" Amalia asks.

"Yup. Fine."

"Do you need to talk?"

You're so preoccupied, you don't hear the words right, most specifically the word YOU. Somehow you're hearing HE, meaning Alex, and you reply, "He does, really badly. But I think he's stopped seeing his therapist."

Amalia's looking at you weirdly. "Not Alex. You."

You laugh and say no, not me, not Good Old Ducky, I don't need to talk. I'm fine. Just have my head in the clouds, that's all.

Because what ELSE can you say — I think my best friend is an alcoholic depressive who hates life? No. It

WOULDN'T BE FAIR TO PUT THAT ON HER. AND IT CERTAINLY WOULDN'T BE FAIR TO ALEX.

So YOU CHAT ABOUT NOTHING AND YOU DROP HER OFF AND YOU PRETEND IT'S A HAP-HAP-HAPPY DAY.

IT'S NOT UNTIL YOU'RE AROUND THE BLOCK THAT YOU START REALIZING HOW GOOD IT WOULD FEEL TO TALK TO AMALIA — TO ANYONE — ABOUT ALL THIS.

AND BECAUSE YOU DON'T — BECAUSE YOU CAN'T — YOU FEEL ROTTEN AND ALONE.

JUST THE RIGHT MOOD FOR YOUR SHIFT AT WINSLOW BOOKS.

ON THE WAY TO THE STORE, YOU STOP AT ALEX'S. PAULA ANSWERS THE DOOR AND TELLS YOU HE'S ASLEEP. So YOU SAY GOOD-BYE AND HEAD TO THE STORE, FEELING RELIEVED THAT AT LEAST HE'S THERE, ALTHOUGH YOU CAN'T IMAGINE WHERE ELSE HE'D BE.

ALEX SPEAKS

YOU CATCH HIM ON THE PHONE AFTER DINNER:

A: "WHAT'S UP, DUCKY?"

D: "HI. NOTHING. I MEAN, I DIDN'T SEE YOU TODAY AT SCHOOL, AND I FIGURED I'D CALL."

A: "Uh-huh."

D: "So...I'm calling! Are you OK?"

A: "As much as I ever am."

D: "I thought...maybe you pulled a muscle or something on the climb. My legs sure are killing me."

A [long pause]: "I'm fine."

D: "You're fine? That's fine. I'm fine too." [Great vocabulary, McCrae.]

A: "Uh, Ducky? You don't have to do this."

D: "What?"

A: "Check up on me. One mother is enough. Just let me have my space."

D: "OK."

You're upbeat. You understand.

But you want to smack yourself because you're making Alex SICK of you — and why shouldn't he be, when you're hovering over him and questioning his every move — and you realize ONCE AGAIN that YOU BETTER WAKE UP, THIS IS YOUR life.

So.

My life...

Let's see. It's fifty-six degrees outside.

The math homework is impossible.

My sneakers are wearing out.

It's almost bedtime.

Thank God.

— Up After Midnight —
This Is Beginning To Become a Habit

Well, bedtime came and went. And you sat there
and tried to think of something ELSE to write, but
you couldn't, so you read and listened to the radio
until you were bored and thirsty, at which point you
headed for the kitchen.

Lo and behold, Ted was there, sneaking a dish of
ice cream, and you grunted hello.

T: "Can't sleep, huh?"

D: "Nope."

T: "Girl trouble?"

(Please.)

D: "Not exactly."

T: "Well, what, exactly?"

D: "Nothing."

T: "Come on, bro, what's on your mind?"

And suddenly you felt like you-know-who, all
bottled up with nowhere to go, which was stupid
because Ted seemed to be in a decent mood, the
kitchen was quiet, and you felt comfortable in a way
you hadn't felt since before Mom and Dad returned,
as if the house was yours again, just the two of you
shooting the breeze at midnight.

You got a glass of water, sank into a kitchen chair, and began to talk — keeping it light, skimming the details, not wanting to bore him — until you realized THIS IS YOUR BROTHER and he's bored you PLENTY over the years, and if you can't talk to him, who, then?

So you unloaded. You talked about Alex's moods, Alex's absences from school, the rock-climbing incident, the way your life had become CONSUMED by Alex's problems.

D: "My best friend is being sucked into his own private black hole, and I'm diving in after him. My other best friends are all eighth-grade girls, and I can't talk to THEM about this. So I keep it to myself. And it affects everything in my life. School. My friendships."

T: "And then, in the middle of all this, Mom and Dad come home."

D: "Right. I felt so strange at the airport, picking them up. Uncomfortable. Same thing at Disneyland. I mean, I should be happy they're home. We're going to be together for Christmas."

T: "Well, life is sometimes like that."

D: "My life, anyway."

T: "Hey, I feel strange about Mom and Dad too. I felt especially strange at Disneyland."

D: "You didn't seem that way. You were acting like a little kid!"

T: "Overcompensation. That's like an exaggerated reaction to cover up how you're really feeling. You'll learn about that in Psych 101."

(Thank you, Dr. Freud.)

D: "So that was an act?"

T: "Sort of. I mean, I feel weird even now. Listen to us, all whispery and quiet. A week ago, we'd be in here crashing around, not worrying about waking anyone up, not caring about who'll notice the food missing from the fridge. It's different now."

Ever since that conversation, you've been thinking about that difference.

Part of you wants everything to be the same. Mom, Dad, Ted, Ducky, apple pie, Disneyland.

But you know it can't be that way again. Not totally.

Before Mom and Dad came home, you'd gotten used to a new life.

Independent. Free.

You hate to admit it, but part of you is looking forward to their next trip.

Tuesday 12/8
Study Hall

    Three tests Friday. You thought they weren't supposed to schedule so many in one day.

    Big trouble. Have to cut this short.

    BTW, Alex in school today. (Hooray.)

    Didn't say much to you, though. Looked tired. As usual.

Late-night Ramblings
Half-open Eyes

    Mom and Dad so quiet during dinner. Dad's mad, I think. Don't know why.

    More details as they become available.

Midweek Checkup
or, The Remains of a Once-Vital Youth:
Ducky, We Hardly Knew Ye

Studied till 11:30 last night. Ouch.

You feel like dry toast today.

Saw Alex at lunch. He must not have seen you. He came in late and took a seat alone by the window. You had dessert with him, but he was very quiet so you didn't force the conversation.

When you went your separate ways afterward, he didn't even say good-bye.

On your way to class, you ran into Sunny, who looked worse than you. She was even more off-the-wall than usual — loud jokes, under-the-breath insults, sudden space-outs.

Poor thing. Her mom's really deteriorating. It's hard to find out exactly how much. Sunny's not giving any straight answers.

But you were worried. So you tracked down Dawn after study hall and asked if she knew anything.

"Sunny doesn't confide in ME anymore," she replied.

Well.

You wish they would patch things up. Sunny desperately needs a best friend.

Don't we all.

Thursday
There's No Place Like Homeroom

Who is DAD to lecture you about bedtimes and study habits?

Now that they're home — NOW you're supposed to suddenly revert to childhood? Get into your jammies and brush your toofies and kiss-kiss before the little hand reaches the nine?

You tried to be calm about it. You ARE a reasonable guy. You explained that 10:45 wasn't too late for a good night's sleep, and you only had twenty more pages to read. And besides, you'd stayed up late OTHER nights this week.

WHY the explosion? WHY?

Something's up. Mom and Dad are arguing behind closed doors — whispering, hissing.

Maybe they're still having trouble adjusting to the return.

Welcome to the club.

Soc Stud

You were walking head down through the main hall, lost in your own world, when you smelled cigarette smoke. You looked up, and you were in the mood to BLAST somebody, to ask the idiot if he could READ THE SIGNS — and you were practically face-to-face with Mrs. Snyder.

She'd just walked through the front door and she was stubbing the butt out in an ashtray.

"Hi," you said.

"Hi," she said.

You probably didn't stand there very long. It just SEEMED that way because you felt so AWKWARD seeing her in the middle of the school day, so you just nodded and moved on while she disappeared into Mr. Dean's office.

Terrific. Alex has become an official Case.

Reflections on a Lousy Day
(Written at Winslow Books)

He totally ignored you at the lockers.

You sat with him at lunch. A half hour of slow chewing and window gazing.

You mentioned you saw his mom. You asked if he saw her.

Shrug. Shrug.

Finally you asked, "Are you mad at me about something?"

He didn't answer. He stood up and left.

How much of this can you take?

Never give up?

NEVER?

Even Good Old Ducky has his limits.

TGIF
Because
YNAW

You Need a Weekend, that is.

Your chemistry exam is a killer.

English and French are no day at the beach either.

In between, you eat lunch all by yourself. Alex is at another table.

Fine.

Unfortunately, Marco and a bunch of Cro Mags sit at the table next to you and start quacking and making stupid comments, turning your lunch into sheer misery.

When the bell rings, you're out of there. But as you're rounding the corner to class, you feel two hands reach around your face and cover your eyes.

You lurch away. You HATE their idiotic pranks and you HATE the fact that ruining your lunch isn't enough, that they have to follow you into the hallway and continue their torture — and you're ready for anything, an egg shampoo, a ridiculous hat, a fight.

But it's Dawn. And behind her is Maggie, holding a flower. And Amalia, with a small box of chocolates.

"Don't EVER do that again!" Great, Ducky, dump on your pals. "I mean, you scared me."

Dawn looks shocked. "Sorry."

"We were going to hold you hostage," Amalia explains. "Force you to endure flowers and chocolate."

"We thought you needed it," Maggie adds.

You feel like a total JERK. You try to smile, but it feels phony. "Thanks, guys."

"I mean, if you don't LIKE chocolate, I'll eat it," Amalia says.

It's a joke. You tell yourself to LIGHTEN UP.

"Whatever," you say. "You can have it."

"Excuse ME, sir," Amalia says, "what have you done with good old Ducky?"

Good Old Ducky.

Good Old, Used-up Ducky.

Discovering Ducky:
A Journey to the Wild, Screaming Beaches

You wind your way among the marauding Rollerbladers.

You shield yourself from the blazing sun.

You risk bruise and blister on the sand and jetties.

And finally you find him. Here on the farthest rock, away from the noisy crowd.

He's floating high over the silver-blue ocean. He's crawling into a cool crevice with the starfish. He's billowing in the sail of a distant catamaran, and he's riding the waves in the wake of the surfers.

You can't really see him. He's not a person, but you wish he were. He's a lot of things you want to be.

He's alone.

He's free.

He's not afraid.

And he knows what's important.

Sunday
Discovering Ducky 2

You fix pancakes for the whole family. Mom is blown away. Dad smiles for the first time since, oh, Tuesday.

Ted says you should have put raisins in the pancakes, but you take it in stride. Cool and good-humored. A rising tide lifts all boats.

Next you call Alex.

He can avoid you all he wants.

HE CAN BE MAD AT YOU.

HE CAN EVEN END THE FRIENDSHIP.

BUT HE HAS TO TALK TO YOU FIRST.

THAT'S ALL YOU ASK.

MRS. SNYDER SAYS HE'S NOT HOME. HE LEFT ON HIS BIKE. SOMEWHERE.

YOU HAVE A HUNCH WHERE.

YOU FIND HIM AT LAS PALMAS COUNTY PARK, AT YOUR OLD SPOT NEAR THE CREEK.

YOU SAY HI AND HE SAYS NADA.

YOU FIGHT THE IMPULSE TO SPIN AWAY AND HEAD RIGHT BACK OVER THE BRIDGE.

YOU DROP YOUR BIKE AND SIT NEXT TO HIM.

D: "IS IT SOMETHING I ATE?"

A [FROWNING]: "WHAT?"

D: "YOU'VE BEEN AVOIDING ME ALL WEEK."

A: "OH. THAT. SORRY."

D: "BODY ODOR, THEN? MY POLITICAL BELIEFS?"

A [NO SMILE. (NO SURPRISE.)]: "I JUST WANTED TO BE ALONE, THAT'S ALL."

D: "YOU CAN'T. I WON'T LET YOU."

A: "DUCKY —"

D: "DO YOU FEEL BETTER WHEN I'M NOT AROUND? DO I MAKE YOU FEEL WORSE?"

A: "NO, BUT —"

D: "I'M NOSY. I TRY TOO HARD. OK. BUT YOU KNOW WHAT? YOU OUGHT TO BE GLAD YOU HAVE A FRIEND LIKE ME."

A: "I AM GLAD."

D: "GOOD. SO LET ME DO WHAT FRIENDS ARE SUPPOSED TO DO. TALK TO ME. STOP TELLING ME NOTHING'S WRONG. I'M CONCERNED ABOUT YOU. I DON'T KNOW IF YOU'RE SEEING DR. WELSCH ANYMORE. I DON'T KNOW IF YOU'RE EVEN TRYING. BUT I WANT TO HELP, ALEX. LET ME. LIFE IS TOO SHORT TO WASTE AWAY."

A [MUMBLES]: "NOT SHORT ENOUGH."

D: "ALEX, STOP IT. YOU SCARE ME WHEN YOU SAY THAT!"

YOU'RE PRACTICALLY SHOUTING. HE DOESN'T REALIZE HOW POWERFUL THOSE WORDS ARE.

A: "OK, DUCKY. OK. YOU'RE RIGHT. I'M SORRY. I'M JUST HAVING A BAD WEEK. THAT'S ALL. AND I AM SEEING DR. WELSCH."

D: "DO YOU TALK TO HIM ABOUT HOW YOU'RE FEELING?"

A: "SURE. BUT I GET KIND OF TALKED OUT. THAT'S WHY I'M SO QUIET. SO DON'T WORRY, OK?"

YOU NOD. BUT YOU'RE NOT REASSURED.

YOU WANT TO TRUST HIM, BUT THAT'S BECOME ALMOST IMPOSSIBLE TO DO.

PART OF YOU THINKS HE'S TELLING YOU WHAT HE THINKS YOU WANT TO HEAR. JUST TO SHUT YOU UP.

AND THAT PART OF YOU IS MAD.

But you don't KNOW. You just don't know.

"Well, I'll be here," you tell him. "You're not going to get rid of me that easily."

Alex nods and smiles faintly. "I hope not."

Holiday Madness
at Winslow Books

That's the sign in the window.

Couldn't they have come up with something better?

It feels weird being here on a Monday. But at school today, Sunny asked you to sub for her.

She caught you in a rare good mood. Why? Because...

You squeaked by with a 78 on the chem, and you managed a B on the English. (You'll find out about French demain.)

So you told Sunny OF COURSE you'll work, but only until 5:30, because dinner's supposed to start early tonight.

Dad has called a Family Meeting.

One can only guess the reason:

→ They've decided to relocate to Palo City permanently.
→ They want Ted and me to move out.
→ They've planned another nostalgic family trip — to the Palo City Nursery School playground.
→ We're all getting bauxite in our stockings for Christmas.

You're tingling with anticipation.

P.S. Alex News:

He was in school today.

Spaced out, as usual.

Although he seemed pretty upbeat, for him. He actually smiled at you. He mentioned how quiet his house will be tonight, because Paula's going to a sleepover party at a friend's. (That's the first he's even mentioned his sister in ages.)

And the last you saw of him, before you rushed off to Winslow Books, he was (gasp) cleaning out his locker.

You're not going to get too excited, though. Don't jump to conclusions — like your talk yesterday actually INFLUENCED him.

He probably just lost something.

And the Hits Keep Coming

That's what it feels like. Another hit to the jaw.
HOW CAN THEY DO THIS?
They gave BIRTH to us. They WANTED to form a family.
What's the point of a family if you can't stay together?
WHAT IS SO SPECIAL ABOUT GHANA?
We were SUPPOSED to have Christmas together. You were looking forward to it. You were going to buy a new botanically correct plastic TREE this weekend. Shop for gifts.

Now what? What can you buy the parents who have EVERYTHING? Who face the IRRESISTIBLE temptation of "exciting research opportunities" in exotic lands, SO exciting that they have to hold a FAMILY MEETING to announce the glad tidings of their imminent departure, and oh, by the way, hold that cheer and 86 the tree, Christmas has been postponed until further notice.

You should have known when you got home from work and saw that the DINING ROOM TABLE had been set up. No kitchen-table dinner for news like this, no sir!

You wish you HAD suspected, because you might have thought of an INTELLIGENT argument, you might have somehow CONVINCED them that they were doing the wrong thing, that it wouldn't KILL them to WAIT until spring or summer OR JUST FIND A JOB CLOSE TO HOME, FOR GOD'S SAKE.

But you didn't.

Instead you just blurted out, "You're leaving before Christmas? You're not even going to be here for THAT?"

Which only made them defensive, and Dad went on and on about how this was a once-in-a-lifetime chance, and hey, the trip's not going to be too long, really, just TWO OR THREE MONTHS, and afterward they'll be home for a long time — besides, Grandma and Grandpa would LOVE to have you and Ted to Pasadena for Christmas, they'll spoil you silly!

"It's not the same!" you said.

Now Dad was sweating and Mom was looking all concerned, but their firm voices and pitying eyes meant they'd talked it out, weighed the options, maybe even reserved the tickets — probably during all those whispered conversations you heard behind doors that were shut solid because YOUR OPINION DOESN'T COUNT.

AND YOU KNEW THAT ARGUING WAS NO USE, THAT YOU WERE TOO EMOTIONAL, YOU WEREN'T GOING TO CONVINCE THEM OF ANYTHING, AND THE BEST YOU COULD DO WAS MAKE THEM FEEL AWFUL.

WHICH YOU DID.

AND THAT WAS JUST FINE.

SO WHAT ARE YOU DOING?

SITTING UP HERE IN YOUR CRAMPED LITTLE ROOM, WRITING YOUR GUTS OUT.

WHILE TED AND MOM AND DAD MUMBLE DOWNSTAIRS.

YOU ARE OUT OF HERE.

~~MON. NIGHT~~

TUES. MORNING

WHATEVER

WHY DO THINGS HAPPEN THE WAY THEY DO?

WHY DO YOU HAVE ARGUMENTS THAT MAKE YOU THINK THE WORLD IS COMING TO AN END, AND YOUR OWN TRIVIAL, STUPID SELF-PITY MAKES YOU RUN AWAY TO A PLACE WHERE THE END OF THE WORLD RUSHES UP TO MEET YOU?

WAS IT FATE THAT YOU WENT TO ALEX'S AFTER YOU

LEFT YOUR HOUSE? OR HAD YOU KNOWN? HAD YOU READ BETWEEN THE LINES AND ANTICIPATED WHAT HAD HAPPENED?

No. DON'T GIVE YOURSELF TOO MUCH CREDIT.

YOU JUST WANTED TO SEE HIM, THAT'S ALL. YOU THOUGHT THAT SOMEWHERE DEEP INSIDE HE'D UNDERSTAND HOW YOU FELT.

HOW HE WAS FEELING HADN'T ENTERED YOUR MIND AT ALL.

YOU JUST RANG AND RANG, BUT NO ONE ANSWERED.

YOU REMEMBERED THAT MRS. SNYDER HAD A BOOK DISCUSSION GROUP ON MONDAY NIGHT. SOMEWHERE IN THE NEIGHBORHOOD. PAULA WAS AT HER SLEEPOVER.

ALEX? ASLEEP PROBABLY.

SO YOU STOMPED BACK OUT TO THE CAR, STILL ANGRY AT MOM AND DAD.

YOU ALMOST DROVE AWAY.

BUT THE NOISE STOPPED YOU. FOR A MOMENT YOU PUT ASIDE YOUR RAGE AND LISTENED.

A CAR ENGINE.

IT SOUNDED FUNNY. MUFFLED. IT WAS COMING FROM THE SNYDERS' DRIVEWAY, BUT THE DRIVEWAY WAS EMPTY.

AND THE GARAGE DOOR WAS CLOSED.

YOUR MIND BLANKED.

BUT YOUR BODY REACTED.

You shot out of the car. Bolted up the driveway. Grabbed the garage handle and pulled.

It was locked.

So you pounded hard. But your only answer was the soft purr of the engine beyond the door.

You raced to the Snyders' back door and yanked up the welcome mat.

You grabbed the spare key, ran back to the garage door, and opened it.

Fumes. Exhaust everywhere.

Your eyes itched. Your lungs filled. You squinted, coughing.

Through the haze you spotted the car-door handle, so you pulled it.

The door swung open.

Smoke wafted out, revealing a leg.

Alex's.

He was sprawled across the backseat.

You dived in. You put your hand to his chest.

It was rising and falling. Slowly.

You reached over the seat, turned off the ignition, then hooked your arms under his and pulled him out. Onto the lawn, away from the exhaust.

You checked for a pulse. There, but barely.

Next thing you knew, you were in the kitchen

calling 911. Maybe the door was open, maybe you used the key, you don't remember.

When the ambulance came, you were slapping Alex's face, shouting his name, trying to revive him.

You were aware that Mrs. Snyder was there too, that she'd arrived just about when the ambulance did, that she was crying and shouting at you — but you weren't hearing her. You were watching Alex. You were seeing the white-sleeved arms lifting him. You were listening to the briskly shouted words, hoping for an encouraging sign. You saw your friend being swallowed up by tubes and straps as he floated on a stretcher into a waiting ambulance whose doors slammed shut, locking him away from you.

Then you were riding with Mrs. Snyder in her car, the windows open to air out the fumes, following the ambulance as it shrieked through the streets, stopping traffic and running red lights.

She pulled into the hospital parking lot in time for you to see him being carried into the building, and one of the technicians had the presence of mind to tell you Alex was alive, he was breathing OK. And you held onto hope even though you were aware of what the technician didn't say — that Alex was going to be all right. That he was going to live.

All you could do was pull yourself together

enough to find the waiting room with Mrs. Snyder, whose face was red and swollen and streaked with tears.

As you sat huddled next to each other on a sofa, the events began replaying in your mind — could you have been quicker, should you have given mouth-to-mouth, should you have dragged him out first and THEN turned off the car?

Mrs. Snyder was sobbing, saying she shouldn't have gone to her book discussion group, she should have stayed home, Alex was acting so strange today, so HAPPY, as if he knew it was all about to end, as if he were looking forward to a trip.

And the word SUICIDE was elbowing its way into your brain — that's what it was, a suicide attempt, your best friend tried to take his own life, and even though you knew that from the moment you found him in the car, it stunned you to finally give a name to what he did.

His words were coming back to you — the hints and signals that now seemed so LOUD AND CLEAR. And you realized that all along, while you thought he wasn't confiding in you, he WAS. He was telling you EVERYTHING. In the muttered comments about life being worthless. In the way he insisted that NOTHING MATTERED. In his refusal to find joy in the obvious

PLACES. Even in his silences he was opening his soul to you, showing you that somehow, for reasons he couldn't understand, it had been emptied.

And today he was cleaning out his locker.

HE WAS CLEANING OUT HIS LOCKER.

Could anything have been more obvious? Did he have to hold a sign up to your face? Write you a good-bye note?

You should have stayed with him then. You should have called Mr. Winslow and told him you couldn't work and spent the day shoulder to shoulder with your best friend until he snapped out of it, no matter how long it took, no matter if it meant taking him yourself to Dr. Welsch.

You told Mrs. Snyder that you should have seen it coming — or maybe she said it to you, you can't remember.

Time passed — five minutes, maybe a half hour, but it seemed like months — and Mrs. Snyder spent most of it on the phone, arranging for Paula to stay at her friend's house for the time being, explaining the situation to the parents but lying like crazy to Paula, telling her Alex had food poisoning. Finally a doctor called you both into a quiet hallway, where he said that Alex was alive and sleeping. His blood and lungs

SHOWED EARLY SIGNS OF CARBON MONOXIDE POISONING, BUT HE
WAS IN STABLE CONDITION.

Stable.

Which is better than critical.

It means he'll live.

The doctor told us we couldn't see Alex yet, he
was still under observation, that we should go home,
get some sleep, and wait for a call in the morning.

You felt a little relieved as you walked back to
the waiting room. You called Mom and Dad from a pay
phone and explained what had happened. You told them
that you wanted to stay until you KNEW Alex was
better. Mom insisted on coming to pick you up.

She arrived a few minutes later. You tried not to
cry but you couldn't help it, you'd been holding it in
all day — and before long Mom's shoulder was wet on
the left side from your tears and on the right from
Mrs. Snyder's.

Mrs. Snyder wanted to wait overnight, in case
Alex woke up and needed her. Mom couldn't convince
her to come back and rest.

So Mom and you left together a little after 10:00.
On the way home, you filled in all the details for her,
and you repeated them to Dad and Ted a few minutes
later, around the kitchen table.

You could barely get the words out, and as you spoke you relived the scene a hundred times, and you HATED when they told you that you'd DONE THE RIGHT THINGS, when they tried to make something POSITIVE out of what was really a botched rescue of a botched life, the last-ditch effort of a friend who listened but never heard, who reacted instead of acted, who stepped in only after it was too late.

No. You don't KNOW it's too late. He may pull through fine.

But what's FINE, Ducky? What's fine for ALEX? Sliding back into the prison of himself? Knowing that the one time he tried to DO something about his situation he FAILED? And now, in addition to the gloom and the emptiness, he'll have to deal with the humiliation that everyone KNOWS what he did?

Will you, Mrs. Snyder, Ms. Krueger, and everyone else who cares about him have to spend each day worrying, monitoring him, suspecting every absence from school, interpreting each change in his attitude, fearing any sudden show of happiness?

Will he be able to live with all that?

Will he try again?

And if he does, will YOU be ready? Will you read the handwriting on the wall when things begin to spin out of control?

How could he DO this? How could ANYONE do something so stupid? Give up a WHOLE LIFE, a hundred thousand sunrises and starry nights and comforts and conflicts and triumphs and dreams? How could he do this to US? DEVASTATE the people who love him. Did he realize that if he'd succeeded, our own lives would be torn apart?

Listen to yourself, Ducky.
You've changed.
No more hopeless optimist.
The OPTIMIST in you would see a silver lining. He'd see that this might be a wake-up call to everyone. That now Alex will get the RIGHT kind of attention. That maybe he's gone as low as he can go, and now he'll start the climb out.
Maybe.
You can only hope.
And be there until it happens.

What a Difference a Night Makes

It's after 3 A.M.
Mom has just left.

She and Dad haven't been able to sleep either.

She told you over and over that you couldn't have done any more than you did. That YOU were the only one who suspected how serious Alex's problem was. That you shouldn't blame yourself for not predicting a suicide attempt. NO ONE wants to believe that will ever happen.

She reminded you that you saved his life. No one else did.

You listened. You tried to let that idea in. You don't know if you can.

Then, as you were thinking, fighting back tears and exhaustion, she took your hand and quietly offered to cancel her travel plans. She and Dad had discussed it and agreed that they didn't HAVE to go to Ghana. They would stay if you needed them around.

You weren't expecting that. And your brain was too fried to even process the idea.

But Mom said not to worry. You didn't have to answer right away. You could think about it.

Sometime.

Like tomorrow.

Today.

Whatever.

Transcript of a Phone Call
at 8 a.m.

Mrs. Snyder: "Is this Ducky?"

Ducky: "Yes! How is he?"

Mrs. S: "Wide-awake. Walking around and talking with the nurses. He's going to make a one hundred percent recovery."

You shout the news. Mom, Dad, and Ted all rush in, relieved.

Mrs. S: "He had JUST passed out when you reached him, Ducky. So the damage wasn't too severe. I hope you realize what you did. I don't know how I can ever repay you."

D: "You can't! I mean, this NEWS is repayment! When is he coming home?"

Mrs. S: "At noon."

D: "TODAY?"

School.

You'll be in school.

You CAN'T.

You can't imagine facing other people today.

You look at Mom and Dad, and they're reading your mind, both nodding yes. Dad's making a gentle palms-down gesture that implies STAY.

Mrs. S: "Ducky, I just spoke to my brother Dave, who's a doctor in Chicago. I told him what happened, and he asked tons of questions — How has Alex behaved? What has he said? It turns out that there are warning signs all of us missed. Signs that can be mistaken for other things, like depression. Alex has some serious problems, Ducky. Things that are beyond all our love and attention. Anyway, Dave's affiliated with a recovery center there, and I've enrolled Alex. I hope to have him on a flight by tonight."

You can't believe it. After all this, Alex is going to be sent away.

D: "Can I come over at noon to talk to him? My mom and dad will let me."

Mrs. S: "Of course. I'd like to see you myself."

11:30
Some Notes About Warning Signs

You've spent much of the last few hours on the Web.

You did a search on teen suicide and downloaded information from some sites.

WHAT ARE THE WARNING SIGNS? THEY'RE SIMILAR TO THE SIGNS OF SEVERE DEPRESSION. NO ONE CAN PREDICT WHEN SEVERE DEPRESSION WILL SPILL INTO A SUICIDE ATTEMPT. SOME STUDIES SHOW THAT THE DESIRE MAY HAVE A CHEMICAL OR GENETIC BASIS. BUT KIDS WHO HAVE TRIED SUICIDE REPORT MANY OF THE SAME SYMPTOMS:

→ CHANGES IN SLEEP HABITS — SLEEPING LATE, DIFFICULTY WAKING, FREQUENT NAPS, CONSTANT YAWNING.

→ WITHDRAWAL FROM FAVORITE ACTIVITIES.

→ WITHDRAWAL FROM FAMILY AND FRIENDSHIPS.

→ INABILITY TO CONCENTRATE.

→ A SUDDEN PERSONALITY CHANGE.

→ DECLINING GRADES.

→ SUBSTANCE ABUSE.

→ HINTS IN CONVERSATION, SUCH AS "NOTHING MATTERS" OR "I WON'T BE A PROBLEM FOR YOU MUCH LONGER."

→ RIGHT BEFORE AN ATTEMPT, A SUDDEN CHEERFULNESS AND/OR A DESIRE TO "PUT THINGS IN ORDER."

YOU LEARNED THAT NONE OF THESE THINGS MEANS THAT A PERSON WILL NECESSARILY ATTEMPT TO KILL HIMSELF. BUT EACH OF THEM IS A SERIOUS SIGN. IT'S ESPECIALLY SERIOUS IF SOMEONE EXHIBITS MORE THAN ONE.

OR ALL.

Like Alex.

You feel as if you're seeing him right up there on the screen.

You print out all the information you can. You file it away in your desk.

Now it's time to go.

You can use the car. Ted and Dad have brought your car back from the Snyders'.

Tuesday afternoon

When you get to the house, he's asleep.

But you don't care.

You're so happy that he's ALIVE. The last time you were here, you thought you'd lost him.

You sit at the kitchen table. Mrs. Snyder fixes you a snack. She asks if you like Oreos and milk and you say yes, but she comes back to the table with orange juice and a box of Wheat Thins.

She's a little out of it. Her hands are shaky, her hair pulled back into a messy ponytail. She looks as if she's been up all night.

She sits across from you and starts speaking softly, painfully:

Mrs. S: "I didn't know, Ducky. I didn't know he was so desperate. I didn't even know he was cutting school until Mr. Dean told me. I leave for work before Alex wakes up, I take care of Paula, who is a handful — and I assumed he was going every day. Alex lied to me about that. He lied about the alcohol too. I knew he was drinking after that awful night you brought him home from Jay's party. I snooped around and found a bottle in his room. Dr. Welsch said that alcoholism wasn't the problem per se, that it was a symptom of depression, but I didn't believe it."

D: "It was impossible to figure him out. I was his closest friend and I didn't know what was wrong."

Mrs. S: "When Mr. Snyder and I divorced, Alex didn't speak for two days. Not a word. I would joke with him, ask him questions — nothing. He didn't seem angry or sad. Just blank. He finally came around a bit, but I don't think he was ever the same."

She goes on and on, recalling more events, remembering angry statements she never should have made, times she should have stayed home from work, hunches she never followed through on.

All her fault. Her fault for divorcing, for having to work two jobs, for not being aggressive enough about getting child support payments, for smoking, for refusing to move to Chicago when her brother

OFFERED HER A JOB, FOR JOINING HER BOOK DISCUSSION GROUP INSTEAD OF STAYING HOME ON MONDAY NIGHTS.

YOUR HEART GOES OUT TO HER. SHE SOUNDS LIKE YOU.

YOU TRY TO REASSURE HER. YOU TELL HER ABOUT SOME OF THE INFORMATION YOU LEARNED ON THE INTERNET — THAT THE SYMPTOMS CAN DECEIVE YOU, THAT YOU CAN'T PREDICT SUICIDAL BEHAVIOR.

MRS. S: "I GUESS YOU CAN DRIVE YOURSELF CRAZY SECOND-GUESSING."

D: "AND IT'S SO HARD TO HELP SOMEONE WHO WON'T TALK. ALEX JUST DETACHED HIMSELF, MRS. SNYDER. FROM SCHOOL. FROM ME. FROM HIS OLD SELF. ON THE ONE HAND, HE INSISTED NOTHING WAS WRONG — AND ON THE OTHER HAND, HE WAS DROPPING ALL THESE HINTS. HOW COULD YOU KNOW WHAT TO TAKE SERIOUSLY? HOW COULD YOU ASSUME YOUR BEST FRIEND, A GUY WHO LOVED LIFE SO MUCH, WOULD EVER THINK OF —"

YOU HAVE TO STOP. MRS. SNYDER IS IN TEARS, AND FINISHING THAT SENTENCE WOULD BE CRUEL.

BUT NOW YOU'RE BREAKING DOWN TOO.

AND SOMETHING ELSE HAPPENS THAT YOU NEVER WOULD HAVE PREDICTED.

SHE OPENS HER ARMS AND HUGS YOU. AND YOU HOLD EACH OTHER, SOBBING SOFTLY, WARMED BY THE MORNING SUNLIGHT THAT STREAMS THROUGH THE KITCHEN WINDOW.

A few moments later, you hear a door open upstairs.

You and Mrs. Snyder go to the bottom landing. Alex is standing in his open doorway. His room is shaded and unlit.

He looks like himself. Somehow, this surprises you.

What were you expecting — gray hair? Electrodes? Maybe just a look of unbearable inner torment.

But he looks unfazed, as if nothing has happened.

"What time is it?" he says with a yawn.

You tell him 12:45. He nods and heads back into his room.

His mom gestures for you to go talk to him, so you climb the stairs.

His room has been tidied up — by Mrs. Snyder, you assume. Alex is lying down on the bedcovers, his eyes half open.

You're nervous. Rigid. What can you say? What does he remember? Should you let him bring it up? Should you be serious? Cheerful? Silent?

You pull out his desk chair and sit next to the bed. Alex speaks first:

A: "Isn't it a school day?"

D: "I stayed home."

A: "You? How come?"

D: "Because of you."

A: "Hey, did you pass that — that English exam?"

D: "French."

A: "Whatever. I knew it was an exam."

D: "I don't know yet. I was supposed to find out today. But it doesn't matter, Alex. I wanted to be here. To see how you're doing."

A: "I'm cool. You didn't have to cut for that."

D: "I'm just so glad you're HERE, Alex. God, I was worried. I couldn't just leave you. Not after last night. So...how do you feel? I mean — why? You know, last night? When did you — what made you do it?"

A: "Ducky, it's no big deal. Really."

The words smack you. They throw you back.

The same old lines. Right back to where you left off.

As if nothing happened.

You seize up. You feel empty. Helpless. The door is slamming shut again and it feels too familiar.

Only now you know what's inside. You know what Alex is holding back.

And you'll be damned if you let him get away with it.

You shout: "How can you say that? How can you possibly say that? Alex, you almost died! I was holding your body. I had to check to see if you were breathing. HOW CAN YOU SAY IT'S NO BIG DEAL? You know what you are, Alex? You're SELFISH. You're a SELFISH and FOOLISH and STUBBORN person who can't take one second to realize that people care about you. I care about you."

You know the words are harsh. You know he's fragile. But there it is. You had to say it.

You don't want praise. You don't want him to fall all over you with thanks. You don't want promises and declarations.

One word is all you need. One word, one LOOK from Alex — some sign that he has heard you, that he understands — and you'll stick around.

Anything less and you'll know it's time to move on. Leave him to the professionals and pray. As hard as that will be.

Not because you hate him. Not because you don't want him to get better.

But because if he can't value the person who saved his life, if he can't show some emotion to the person who knows his deepest secret, then that person means nothing to him.

And you can't be nothing.

So you lock eyes with him, waiting for an answer. But he turns away, his face still as stone.

You stand quietly.

And then you leave.

Mrs. Snyder is staring at you as you walk through the house. You meet her glance briefly, painfully, but you keep going.

You hear her running up the stairs as you head out the door.

You climb into your car, steeling yourself against tears. You turn on the ignition and shift into drive.

"Ducky! Wait!"

Mrs. Snyder is running toward you across the lawn.

You lower the passenger window, and she leans in. "Alex told me he wants to speak to you. Please don't go."

You feel numb as you turn the car off. Numb as you walk toward the house. Numb as you enter and climb the stairs.

Alex's bedroom door is open.

His back is to you. He's looking out the window.

You stand for a moment, but he doesn't move.

So you walk closer.

And you see that he's crying.

"Alex?" you say.

His face, so blank and unfeeling a moment ago,

now looks sunken and hollow. When he speaks, you can barely hear him.

"I'm sorry," he says. "I'm so sorry."

You feel your own rage washing away. You reach out and put a hand on his shoulder. "Just get better," you whisper back.

He raises his eyes to the big sycamore tree in the front yard. A faint smile plays across his face. "You know what I thought of last night in the hospital? The time I fell out of that tree."

You cringe at the memory. You were only ten. You stood there, helpless, while he howled and howled. "I remember."

"The pain was unbelievable. I never imagined ANYTHING could hurt so much."

"I'd never heard you scream like that."

"Well, last night I thought about how falling out of the tree was nothing compared to this."

Finally Alex turns toward you.

He's looking you straight in the eye.

You understand.

Totally.

And you see why he couldn't open up.

It wasn't your fault.

Or his.

Opening up meant feeling that pain.

So he buried it inside. Until he couldn't bury it anymore.

You sit at the foot of his bed. He sits on the pillow. The way you've sat a million other times for a million other conversations.

He talks a little about Chicago. He's dreading it in a way, but looking forward to a change of scenery.

You tell him to bring back Frango mints. Whenever Mom and Dad go to Chicago, they always bring back Frango mints from some big department store.

It's a dumb thing to say, but it feels right.

Alex promises he'll find some.

You help him pull down a suitcase from his closet shelf. You both begin packing his stuff. His mom comes upstairs and reminds Alex that they have to leave soon to pick up his ticket at the airport.

"I've got it under control now," Alex says to you. About the packing.

"Well," you reply.

"Yeah," he says. "I'll see you soon."

"Call me."

"I will."

You turn to leave, but before you're out the door, Alex mumbles, "Thank you." Then he continues packing.

And you leave.

As you walk down the stairs, you feel dazed.

You try not to think that you almost threw away your friendship.

He was the one who pulled you back.

But in a way, that was how it should have been.

After so much blindness and bumbling, after everything you've done wrong, at least you know you did one thing right.

Thursday 12/17
Los Angeles International Airport
in which Ducky Returns After a Two-Day Rest

Some rest.

Between school, homework, phone conversations with Mrs. Snyder, e-mail to Alex, preparations for Mom and Dad's trip, and taking them to meet the plane, you haven't stopped.

Telling Mom and Dad they should go to Ghana was the hardest part of the last two days.

You reached that decision in the car, on the way back from Alex's on Tuesday.

What was the point of their staying home? Alex is

GOING TO BE AWAY. YOU'LL BE FINE. ALL THEY'D BE DOING WOULD BE MOPING AROUND THE HOUSE, THINKING ABOUT THE TRIP THEY DIDN'T TAKE.

TED AND YOU CAN BUY THE BOTANICALLY CORRECT TREE AND CELEBRATE A BROTHERLY CHRISTMAS. YOU'LL MAKE IT FUN.

MOM AND DAD KEPT ASKING IF YOU WERE SURE, INSISTING THEY'D BE HAPPY TO STAY. YOU KNEW THEY WERE SINCERE. BUT YOU COULD SENSE THEIR RELIEF. AND THEIR APPRECIATION.

DRIVING TO THE AIRPORT, YOU WERE TOTALLY FINE. SAYING GOOD-BYE, THOUGH, WAS A DIFFERENT STORY. FOR THE FIRST TIME SINCE YOU WERE A LITTLE BOY, YOU CRIED. YOU NEVER THOUGHT YOU'D MISS THEM SO MUCH.

THEY CRIED BACK. YOU HUGGED EACH OTHER UNTIL THE FINAL BOARDING ANNOUNCEMENT. AND YOU STOOD BY THE WINDOW AND WAVED TO THE PLANE AS IT TOOK OFF.

THE WAY YOU DID WHEN YOU WERE LITTLE.

EVERYTHING'S CHANGED SO MUCH SINCE THE DAY YOU PICKED THEM UP HERE. YOU'VE CHANGED.

AS A SON.

AS A BROTHER.

AS A FRIEND.

YOU FEEL FUNNY ABOUT GOING BACK TO PALO CITY NOW. TO LIFE WITHOUT PARENTS.

OR ALEX.

When he called you from Chicago this afternoon, he didn't say much. But he sounded a little upbeat, I think. He said he hopes to come home soon.

You talked to Mrs. Snyder afterward. She thinks he sounds "fragile."

She's not so sure about the coming-home-soon part.

Neither am I.

Oh, well. I guess it'll be pretty lonely for awhile.

At least I have Ted. And my friends.

They'll be glad Good Old Ducky's back.

I'm not sure I'm up to being Good Old Ducky just yet, though.

Maybe just plain Ducky.

If I can figure out who that is.

I. GODWIN

Ann M. Martin

About the Author

ANN MATTHEWS MARTIN was born on August 12, 1955. She grew up in Princeton, NJ, with her parents and her younger sister, Jane.

Although Ann used to be a teacher and then an editor of children's books, she's now a full-time writer. She gets the ideas for her books from many different places. Some are based on personal experiences. Others are based on childhood memories and feelings. Many are written about contemporary problems or events.

All of Ann's characters are made up. But some of her characters are based on real people. Sometimes Ann names her characters after people she knows; other times she chooses names she likes.

In addition to California Diaries, Ann Martin has writen many other books, including the Baby-sitters Club series. She has written twelve novels for young people, including *Missing Since Monday*, *With You or Without You*, *Slam Book*, and *Just a Summer Romance*.

Ann M. Martin does not live in California, though she does visit frequently. She lives in New York with her cats, Gussie and Woody. Her hobbies are reading, sewing, and needlework—especially making clothes for children.

CALIFORNIA DIARIES

Look for #11

DAWN, DIARY THREE

Saturday morning 2/20
9:02

I cannot go to the concert with Sunny. I just can't.

Saturday morning 2/20
9:07

Not go to see Jax live? Not see Pierre in person? I must be crazy. Of course I'm going to go.

Saturday morning 2/20
9:10

With SUNNY????

Saturday evening 2/20

   I have been thinking about the Sunny
dilemma all day. Obsessively. I've
thought about it way more than about
having to ask Dad and Carol for per-
mission to go to the concert in the first
place. Maybe I should worry about _that_
instead. After all, the concert is in just
13 days. I have a lot of work to do.

Saturday night 2/20
10:42

   13 NIGHTS FROM RIGHT NOW I
WILL BE IN THE SAME ROOM
WITH JAX AND PIERRE X!!!!!

SATURDAY NIGHT 2/20
10:44

If Dad and Carol let me go.

Life is changing. Fast.

New scents. New problems....
Her helps....

California Diaries

From Best-selling Author
ANN M. MARTIN